Joseph Sheridan Le Fanu

The Wyvern Mystery

A Novel: Vol. II.

Joseph Sheridan Le Fanu

The Wyvern Mystery
A Novel: Vol. II.

ISBN/EAN: 9783337032951

Printed in Europe, USA, Canada, Australia, Japan

Cover: Foto ©Andreas Hilbeck / pixelio.de

More available books at **www.hansebooks.com**

THE WYVERN MYSTERY.

A Novel.

By J. S. LE FANU,

AUTHOR OF "UNCLE SILAS," "GUY DEVERELL," ETC., ETC.

IN THREE VOLUMES.

VOL. II.

LONDON :

TINSLEY BROTHERS, 18, CATHERINE ST., STRAND.

1869.

LONDON:
BRADBURY, EVANS, AND CO., PRINTERS, WHITEFRIARS.

CONTENTS.

CONTENTS.

THE WYVERN MYSTERY.

CHAPTER I.

THE SUMMONS.

WHEN Charles Fairfield came into the wainscoted dining-room a few minutes later it looked very cosy. The sun had broken the pile of western clouds, and sent low and level a red light flecked with trembling leaves on the dark panels that faced the windows.

Outside in that farewell glory of the day the cawing crows were heard returning to the sombre woods of Carwell, and the small birds whistled and warbled pleasantly in the clear air, and chatty sparrows in the ivy round gossiped and fluttered merrily before the little community betook themselves to their leafy nooks and couched their busy little heads for the night under their brown wings.

He looked through the window towards the gloriously-stained sky and darkening trees, and he thought,—

"A fellow like me, who has seen out his foolish days and got to value better things, who likes a pretty view, and a cigar, and a stroll by a trout-brook, and a song now and then, and a book, and a friendly guest, and a quiet glass of wine, and who has a creature like Alice to love and be loved by, might be devilish happy in this queer lonely corner, if only the load were off his heart."

He sighed; but something of that load was for the moment removed; and as pretty Alice came in at the open door, he went to meet her, and drew her fondly to his heart.

"We must be very happy this evening, Alice. Somehow I feel that everything will go well with us yet. If just a few little hitches and annoyances were got over, I should be the happiest fellow, I think, that ever bore the name of Fairfield ; and you, darling creature, are the light of that happiness. My crown and my life—my beautiful Alice, my joy and my glory—I wish you knew half how I love you, and how proud I am of you."

"Oh, Charlie, Charlie, this is delightful. Oh, Ry, my darling ! I'm too happy."

And with these words, in the strain of her slender embrace, she clung to him as he held her locked to his heart.

The affection was there ; the love was true. In the indolent nature of Charles Fairfield capabilities of good were not wanting. That dreadful interval in the soul's history, between the weak and comparatively noble state of childhood and that later period when experience saddens and illuminates and begins to turn our looks regretfully backward, was long past with him. The period when women "come out" and see the world, and men in the old-fashioned phrase "sow their wild oats"—that glorious summer-time of self-love, sin, and folly—that bleak and bitter winter of the soul, through which the mercy of God alone preserves for us alive the dormant germs of good, was past for him, without killing, as it sometimes does, all the tenderness and truth of the nursery. In this man, Charles Fairfield, were the trodden-down but still living affections which now, in this season, unfolded themselves anew—simplicity unkilled, and the purity not of Eden, not of childhood, but of *recoil*. Altogether a man who had not lost himself—capable of being happy—capable of being regenerated.

I know not exactly what had evoked this sudden glow and effervescence. Perhaps it needs some manifold confluence of internal and external conditions, trifling and unnoticed, except for such unexplained results, to evolve these tremblings and lightings up that surprise us like the fiercer analogies of volcanic chemistry.

It is sad to see what appear capabilities and opportunities of a great happiness so nearly secured, and yet by reason of some inflexible caprice of circumstance quite unattainable.

It was not for some hours, and until after his wife had gone to her room, that the darkness and chill that portended the return of his worst care crept over him as he sat and turned over the leaves of his book.

He got up and loitered discontentedly about the room. Stopping now before the little book-shelves between the windows and adjusting unconsciously their contents; now at the little oak table, and fiddling with the flowers which Alice had arranged in a tall old glass, one of the relics of other days of Carwell; and so on, listless, irresolute.

"So here I am once more—back again among my enemies! Happiness for me, a momentary illusion — hope a cheat. My *reality* is the blackness of the abyss. God help me!"

He turned up his eyes, and he groaned this prayer, unconscious that it was a prayer.

"I will," he thought, "extract the sting from this miserable mystery. Between me and Alice it shall be a secret no longer. I'll tell her to-morrow. I'll look out an opportunity; I will by——"

And to nail himself to his promise this irresolute man repeated the same passionate oath, and he struck his hand on the table.

Next day, therefore, when Alice was again among the flowers in the garden he entered that antique and solemn shade with a strange sensation at his heart of fear and grief. How would Alice · look on him after it was over? How would she bear it?

Pale as the man who walks after the coffin of his darling, between the tall gray piers he entered that wild and umbrageous enclosure.

His heart seemed to stop still as he saw little Alice, all unsuspicious of his dreadful message, working with her tiny trowel at the one sunny spot of the garden.

She stood up—how pretty she was!—looking on her work ; and as she stood with one tiny foot advanced, and her arms folded, with her garden-gloves on, and the little diamond-shaped trowel glittering in her hand, she sang low to herself an air which he remembered her singing when she was quite a little thing long ago at Wyvern—when he never dreamed she would be anything to him —just a picture of a little brown-haired girl and nothing dearer.

Then she saw him, and—

"Oh, Ry, darling !" she cried, as making a diagonal from the distant point, she ran towards him through tall trees and old raspberries, and under the boughs of over-grown fruit trees, which now-a-days bore more moss and lichen than pears or cherries upon them.

"Ry, how delightful ! You so seldom come here, and now I have you, you shall see all

I'm doing, and how industrious I have been ;
and we are going to have such a happy little
ramble. Has anything happened, darling ? "
she said, suddenly stopping and looking in
his face.

Here was an opportunity ; but if his resolution was still there, presence of mind failed
him, and forcing a smile, he instantly answered—

"Nothing, darling — nothing whatever.
Come, let us look at your work ; you are so
industrious, and you have such wonderful
taste."

And as, reassured, and holding his hand,
she prattled and laughed, leading him round
by the grass-grown walks to her garden, as
she called that favoured bit of ground on
which the sun shone, he hardly saw the
old currant bushes or gray trunks of the
rugged trees ; his sight seemed dazzled ; his
hearing seemed confused ; and he thought to
himself—

"Where am I—what is this—and can it

be true that I am so weak or so mad as to be
turned from the purpose over which I have
been brooding for a day and a night, and to
which I had screwed my courage so reso-
lutely, by a smile and a question—What is
this?   Black currant; and this is groundsel;
and little Alice, your glove wants a stitch or
two," he added aloud; "and oh! here we
are.   Now you must enlighten me; and
what a grove of little sticks, and little
inscriptions.   These are your annuals, I
suppose?"

And so they talked, and she laughed and
chatted very merrily, and he had not the
heart—perhaps the courage—to deliver his
detested message; and again it was post-
poned.

The next day Charles Fairfield fell into his
old gloom and anxieties; the temporary
relief was felt no more, and the usual reaction
followed.

It is something to have adopted a resolution.   The anguish of suspense, at least, is

ended, and even if it be to undergo an operation, and to blow one's own brains out, men will become composed, and sometimes even cheerful, as the coroner's inquest discovers, when once the way and the end are known.

But this melancholy serenity now failed Charles Fairfield, for without acknowledging it, he began a little to recede from his resolution. Then was the dreadful question, how will she bear it, and even worse, how will she view the position? Is she not just the person to leave forthwith a husband thus ambiguously placed, and to insist that this frightful claim, however shadowy, should be met and determined in the light of day?

"I know very well what an idol she makes of me, poor little thing; but she would not stay here an hour after she heard it; she would go straight to Lady Wyndale. It would break her heart, but she would do it."

It was this fear that restrained him. Impelling him, however, was the thought that, sooner or later, if Harry's story were true, his enemy would find him out, and his last state be worse than his first.

Again and again he cursed his own folly for not having consulted his shrewd brother before his marriage. How horribly were his words justified. How easy it would have been comparatively to disclose all to Alice before leading her into such a position. He did not believe that there was actual danger in this claim. He could swear that he meant no villany. Weak and irresolute, in a trying situation, he had been—that was all. But could he be sure that the world would not stigmatize him as a villain ?

Another day passed, and he could not tell what a day might bring—a day of feverish melancholy, of abstraction, of agitation.

She had gone to her room. It was twelve o'clock at night, when, having made up his mind to make his agitating shrift, he mounted the old oak stairs, with his candle in his hand.

"Who's there?" said his wife's voice from the room.

"I, darling."

And at the door she met him in her dressing-gown. Her face was pale and miserable, and her eyes swollen with crying.

"Oh, Ry, darling, I'm so miserable; I think I shall go mad."

And she hugged him fast in trembling arms, and sobbed convulsively on his breast.

Charles Fairfield froze with a kind of terror. He thought, "she has found out the whole story." She looked up in his face, and that was the face of a ghost.

"Oh, Ry, darling, for God's sake tell me— is there anything very bad—is it debt only that makes you so wretched; I am in such dreadful uncertainty. Have mercy on your poor little miserable wife, and tell me what-ever it is—tell me all!"

Here you would have said was something

more urgent than the opportunity which he coveted ; but the sight of that gaze of wildest misery smote and terrified him, it looked in reality so near despair, so near insanity.

"To tell her will be to kill her," something seemed to whisper, and he drew her closer to him, and kissed her and laughed.

"Nothing on earth but money—the want of money — debt. Upon my soul you frightened me, Alice, you looked so, so piteous. I thought you had something dreadful to tell me ; but, thank God, you are quite well, and haven't even seen a ghost. You must not always be such a foolish little creature. I'm afraid this place will turn our heads. Here we are safe and sound, and nothing wrong but my abominable debts. You would not wonder at my moping if you knew what debt is ; but I won't look, if I can help it, quite so miserable for the future ; for, after all, we must have money soon, and you know they can't hang me for owing them a few hundreds ; and I'm quite angry with myself for having annoyed you so, you poor little thing,"

" My noble Ry, it is so good of you, you make me so happy, I did not know what to think, but you have made me quite cheerful again, and I really do think it is being so much alone, I watch your looks so much, and everything prays on me so, and that seems so odious when I have my darling along with me ; but Ry will forgive his foolish little wife, I know he will, he's always so good and kind."

Then followed more re-assuring speeches from Charles, and more raptures from poor Alice. And the end was that for a time Charles was quite turned away from his purpose. I don't know, however, that he was able to keep his promise about more cheerful looks, certainly not beyond a day or two.

A few days later he heard a tragic bit of news. Tom related to him that the miller's young wife, down at Raxleigh, hearing on a

sudden that her husband was drowned in the
mill-stream, though 'twas nothing after all
but a ducking, was " took wi' fits, and died in
three days time."

So much for surprising young wives with
alarming stories ! Charles Fairfield listened,
and made the application for himself.

A few days later a letter was brought into
the room, where rather silently Charles and
his wife were at breakfast. It came when he
had almost given up the idea of receiving one
for some days, perhaps weeks, and he had
begun to please himself with the idea that
the delay augured well, and Harry's silence
was a sign that the alarm was subsiding.

Here, however, was a letter addressed to
him in Harry's bold hand. His poor little
wife sitting next the tea things, eyed her
husband as he opened it, with breathless
alarm ; she saw him grow pale as he glanced
at it ; he lowered it to the table cloth, and
bit his lip, his eye still fixed on it.

As he did not turn over the leaf, she saw

it could not be a long one, and must all be comprised within one page.

"Ry, darling," she asked, also very pale, in a timid voice, "it's nothing very bad. Oh, darling, what is it?"

He got up and walked to the window silently.

"What do you say, darling?" he asked, suddenly, after a little pause.

She repeated her question.

"No, darling, nothing, but—but possibly we may have to leave this. You can read it, darling."

He laid the letter gently on the tablecloth beside her, and she picked it up, and read—

"MY DEAR CHARLIE,

"The old soldier means business. I think you must go up to London, but be sure to meet me to-morrow at Hatherton, say the Commercial Hotel, at four o'clock, P.M.

"Your affectionate brother,

"HARRY FAIRFIELD."

"Who does he mean by the old soldier?' asked Alice, very much frightened, after a silence.

"One of those d——d people who are plaguing me," said Charles, who had returned to the window, and answered, still looking out.

"And what is his real name, darling?"

"I'm ashamed to say that Harry knows ten times as well as I all about my affairs. I pay interest through his hands, and he watches those people's movements; he's a rough diamond, but he has been very kind, and you see his note—where is it? Oh, thanks. I must be off in half an hour, to meet the coach at the ' Pied Horse.' "

"Let me go up, darling, and help you to pack, I know where all your things are," said poor little Alice, who looked as if she was going to faint.

"Thank you, darling, you are such a good

little creature, and never think of yourself—
never, never—*half enough.*"

His hands were on her shoulders, and he
was looking in her face, with sad strange
eyes, as he said this, slowly, like a man
spelling out an inscription.

"I wish—I wish a thousand things. God
knows how heavy my heart is. If you cared
for yourself Alice, like other women, or that
I weren't a fool—but—but you, poor little
thing, it was such a venture, such a sea, such
a crazy boat to sail in."

"I would not give up my Ry, my darling,
my husband, my handsome, clever, noble Ry
—I'd lose a thousand lives if I had them, one
by one, for you, Charlie ; and oh, if you left
me, I should die."

"Poor little thing," he said, drawing her
to him with a trembling strain, and in his
eyes, unseen by her, tears were standing.

"If you leave this, won't you take me,
Charlie ? won't you let me go wherever you
go ? and oh, if they take my man—I'm to go

with you, Charlie, promise that, and oh, my darling, you're not sorry you married your poor little Alley."

"Come, darling, come up ; you shall hear from me in a day or two, or see me. This will blow over, as so many other troubles have done," he said, kissing her fondly.

And now began the short fuss and confusion of a packing on brief notice, while Tom harnessed the horse, and put him to the dog-cart.

And the moment having arrived, down came Charles Fairfield, and Tom swung his portmanteau into its place, and poor little Alice was there with, as Old Dulcibella said, " her poor little face all cried," to have a last look, and a last word, her tiny feet on the big unequal paving stones, and her eyes following Charlie's face, as he stepped up and arranged his rug and coat on the seat, and then jumped down for the last hug ; and the wild, close, hurried whisperings, last words of love and cheer from laden hearts, and pale

smiles, and the last, *really* the last look, and
the dog-cart and Tom, and the portmanteau
and Charlie, and the sun's blessed light, dis-
appear together through the old gateway
under the wide stone arch, with tufted ivy and
careless sparrows, and little Alice stands alone
on the pavement for a moment, and runs
out to have one last wild look at the disap-
pearing "trap," under the old trees, as it
rattled swiftly down to the narrow road of
Carwell Valley.

It vanished—it was gone—the tinkling of
the wheels was heard no more. The parting,
for the present, was quite over, and poor little
Alice turned at last, and threw her arms
about the neck of kind old Dulcibella, who
had held her when a baby in her arms in the
little room at Wyvern Vicarage, and saw her
now a young wife, " wooed and married, and
a'," in the beauty and the sorrows of life ;
and the light air of autumn rustled in the
foliage above her, and a withered leaf or two
fell from the sunlit summits to the shadow at

her feet; and the old woman's kind eyes
filled with tears, and she whispered homely
comfort, and told her she would have him
back again in a day or two, and not to take
on so; and with her gentle hand, as she em-
braced her, patted her on the shoulder, as she
used in other years—that seemed like yesterday—to comfort her in nursery troubles.
But our sorrows outgrow their simple con-
solations, and turn us in their gigantic
maturity to the sympathy and wisdom that is
sublime and eternal.

Days passed away, and a precious note
from Charlie came. It told her where to
write to him in London, and very little
more.

The hasty scrawl added, indeed em-
phatically, that she was to tell his address
to no one. So she shut it up in the
drawer of the old-fashioned dressing-table,
the key of which she always kept with
her.

Other days passed. The hour was dull at

Carwell Grange for Alice. But things moved on in their dull routine without event or alarm.

Old Mildred Tarnley was sour and hard as of old, and up to a certain time neither darker nor brighter than customary. Upon a day, however, there came a shadow and a fear upon her.

Two or three times on that day and the next, was Mrs. Tarnley gliding, when old Dulcibella with her mistress was in the garden, about Alice's bed-room, noiselessly as a shadow. The little girl downstairs did not know where she was. It was known but to herself—and what she was about. Coming down those dark stairs, and going up, she went on tiptoe, and looked black and stern as if she was "laying out" a corpse upstairs.

Accidentally old Dulcibella, coming into the room on a message from the garden, surprised lean, straight Mrs. Tarnley, feloniously trying to turn a key, from a bunch in her hand, in the lock of the dressing-table drawer.

"Oh, la! Mrs. Tarnley," cried old Dulcibella, very much startled.

The two women stood perfectly still, staring at one another. Each looked scared. Stiff Mildred Tarnley, without, I think, being the least aware of it, dropped a stiff short courtesy, and for some seconds more the silence continued.

"What *be* you a-doing here, Mrs. Tarnley?" at length demanded Dulcibella Crane.

"No occasion to tell *you*," replied Mildred, intrepidly. "Another one, that owed her as little as I'm like ever to do, would tell your young mistress. But I don't want to break her heart—what for should I? There's dark stories enough about the Grange without no one hangin' theirself in their garters. What I want is where to direct a letter to Master Charles—that's all."

"I can't say, I'm sure," said old Dulcibella.

"She got a letter from him o' Thursday last; 'twill be in it no doubt, and that I take it, ma'am, is in this drawer, for she used not to lock it; and I expect you, if ye love your young mistress, to help me to get at it," said Mrs. Tarnley, firmly.

"Lor, Mrs. Tarnley, ma'am! *me* to pick a lock, ma'am! I'd die first. Ye can't mean it?"

"I knowd ye was a fool. I shouldn't 'a said nothing to ye about it," said Mildred, with sharp disdain.

"Lawk! I never was so frightened in my life!" responded Dulcibella.

"Ye'll be more so, mayhap. I wash my hands o' ye," said Mrs. Tarnley, with a furious look, and a sharp little stamp on the floor. "I thought o' nothing but your mistress's good, and if ye tell her I was here, I'll explain all, for I won't lie under no surmises, and I think 'twill be the death of her."

"Oh, this place, this hawful place! I never

was so frightened in my days," said Dulcibella,
looking very white.

"She's in the garden now, I do suppose,"
said Mildred, "and if ye mean to tell her
what I was about, 'taint a pin's head to me,
but I'll go out and tell her myself, and even
if she lives through it, she'll never hold up
her head more, and that's all *you'll* hear from
Mildred Tarnley."

"Oh, dear! dear! dear! my heart, how it
goes!"

"Come, come, woman, you're nothin' so
squeamish, I dare say."

"Well," said Dulcibella; "it may be all as
you say, ma'am, and I'll say ye this justice, I
ha'n't missed to the value of a pennypiece
since we come here, but if ye promise me,
only ye won't come up here no more while
we're out, Mrs. Tarnley, I won't say nothing
about it."

"That settles it, keep your word, Mrs.
Crane, and I'll keep mine; I'll burn my
fingers no more in other people's messes;'

and she shook the key with a considerable
gingle of the whole bunch from the keyhole,
and popped it grimly into her pocket.

" Your sarvant, Mrs. Crane."

" Yours, Mrs. Tarnley, ma'am," replied
Dulcibella.

And the interview which had commenced
so brusquely, ended with ceremony, as Mildred
Tarnley withdrew.

That old woman was in a sort of fever that
afternoon and the next day, and her temper,
Lilly Dogger thought, grew more and more
savage as night approached. She had in her
pocket a friendly fulsome little letter, which
had reached her through the post, announcing
an arrival for the night that was now approaching. The coach that changed horses
at the " Pied Horse," was due there at half-
past eleven, P.M., but might not be there till
twelve, and then there was a long drive to
Carwell Grange.

" I'm wore out wi' them, I'm tired to
death ; I'm wore off my feet wi' them ; I'm

worked like a hoss. 'Twould be well for Mildred Tarnley, I'm thinkin', she was under the mould wi' a stone at her head, and shut o' them all."

CHAPTER II.

THAT night the broad-shouldered child, Lilly Dogger, was up later than usual. An arrear of pots and saucepans to scour, along with customary knives and forks to clean, detained her.

"Bustle, you huzzy, will ye?" cried the harsh voice of old Mildred, who was adjusting the kettle on the kitchen fire, while in the scullery the brown-eyed little girl worked away at the knife-board. A mutton-fat, fixed in a tin sconce on the wall, so as to command both the kitchen and the scullery, economically lighted each, the old woman and her drudge, at her work.

"Yes'm, please," she said, interrogatively,

for the noise of her task prevented her hearing distinctly.

"Be alive, I say. It's gone eleven, you slut; ye should a bin in your bed an hour," screeched Mildred, and then relapsed into her customary grumble.

"Yes, Mrs. Tarnley, please'm," answered the little girl, resuming with improved energy.

Drowsy enough was the girl. If there had been a minute's respite from her task, I think she would have nodded.

"Be them things rubbed up or no, or do you mean to 'a done to-night, huzzy?" cried Mrs. Tarnley, this time so near as to startle her, for she had unawares put her wrinkled head into the scullery. "Stop that for to-night, I say. Leave 'em lay, ye'll finish in the morning."

"Shall I take down the fire, Mrs. Tarnley, ma'am, please?" asked Lilly Dogger, after a little pause.

"No, ye shan't. What's that ye see on

the fire ; have ye eyes in your head ? Don't ye see the kettle there ? How do I know but your master'll be home to-night, and want a cup o' tea, or—law knows what ?"

Mrs. Tarnley looked put about, as she phrased it, and in one of those special tempers which accompanied that state. So Lilly Dogger, eyeing her with wide open eyes, made her a frightened little courtesy.

"Why don't ye get up betimes in the morning, huzzy, and then ye needn't be mopin' about half the night ? All the colour's washed out o' your big, ugly, platter face, wi' your laziness—as white as a turnip. When I was a girl, if I left my work over so, I'd 'a the broomstick across my back, I promise ye, and bread and water next day too good for my victuals ; but now ye thinks ye can do as ye like, and all's changed! An' every upstart brat is as good as her betters. But don't ye think ye'll come it over me, lass, don't ye. Look up there at the clock, will ye, or do ye want me to pull

ye up by the ear—ten minutes past eleven—
wi' your dawdling, ye limb!"

The old woman whisked about, and putting
her hand on a cupboard door, she turned
round again before opening it, and said—

"Come on, will ye, and take your bread
if you want it, and don't ye stand gaping
there, ye slut, as if I had nothing to do
but attend upon you, with your impittence.
I shouldn't give ye *that*."

She thumped a great lump of bread down
on the kitchen table by which the girl was
now standing.

"Not a bit, if I did right, and ye'll not be
sittin' up to eat that, mind ye; ye'll take it
wi' ye to yer bed, young lady, and tumble in
without delay, d'ye mind? For if I find ye
out o' bed when I go in to see all's right, I'll
just gi'e ye that bowl o' cold water over yer
head. In wi' ye, an' get ye twixt the blankets
before two minutes—get along."

The girl knew that Mrs. Tarnley could
strike as well as "jaw," and seldom threatened

in vain, so with eyes still fixed upon her, she took up her fragment of loaf, with a hasty courtesy, of which the old woman took no notice, and vanished frightened through a door that opened off the kitchen.

The old woman holding the candle over her head, soon peeped in as she had threatened.

Lilly Dogger lay close affecting to be asleep, though that feat in the time was impossible, and was afraid that the thump, thump of her heart, for she greatly feared Mrs. Tarnley, might be audible to that severe listener.

Out she went, however, without anything more, to the great relief of the girl.

Lilly Dogger lay awake, for fear is vigilant, and Mrs. Tarnley's temper she knew was capricious as well as violent.

Through the door she heard the incessant croak of the old woman's voice, as she grumbled and scolded in soliloquy, poking here and there about the kitchen. The girl lay awake, listening vaguely in the dark, and watching the one bright spot on the whitewashed wall at the foot of her bed, which Mrs. Tarnley's candle in the kitchen transmitted through the keyhole. It flitted and glided, now hither, now thither, now up, now down, like a white butterfly in a garden, silently indicating the movements of the old woman, and illustrating the clatter of her clumsy old shoes.

In a little while the door opened again, and the old woman entered, having left her candle on the dresser outside.

Mrs. Tarnley listened for a while, and you may be sure Lilly Dogger lay still. Then the old woman in a hard whisper asked, "Are you awake?" and listened.

"Are ye awake, lass?" she repeated, and receiving no answer she came close to the bed, by way of tucking in the coverlet, in reality to listen.

So she stood in silence by the bed for a minute, and then very quickly withdrew and closed the door.

Then Lilly Dogger heard her make some

arrangements in the kitchen, and move, as she rightly concluded, a table which she placed against her door.

Then the white butterfly having made a sudden sweep round the side wall, hovered no longer on Lilly Dogger's darkened walls, and old Mildred Tarnley and her candle glided out of the kitchen.

The girl had grown curious, and she got up and peeped, and found that a clumsy little kitchen table had been placed against her door, which opened outward.

Through the keyhole she also saw that Mildred had not taken down the fire. On the contrary, she had trimmed and poked it, and a kettle was simmering on the bar.

She did not believe that Mrs. Tarnley expected the arrival of her master, for she had said early in the day that she thought he would come next evening. Lilly Dogger was persuaded that Mrs. Tarnley was on the look out for some one else, and guarding that fact with a very jealous secrecy.

She went again to her bed; wondering
she listened for the sounds of her return, and
looked for the little patch of light on the
whitewashed wall; but that fluttering evidence of Mrs. Tarnley's candle did not re-
appear before the tired little girl fell asleep.

She was wakened in a little time by Mrs.
Tarnley's somewhat noisy return. She was
grumbling bitterly to herself, poking the fire,
and pitching the fire-irons and other hard-
ware about with angry recklessness.

The girl turned over, and notwithstanding
all Mildred's noisy soliloquy was soon asleep
again.

Again she awoke—I suppose recalled to
consciousness by some noise in the kitchen.
The little white light was in full play on
the wall at the foot of her bed, and Mrs.
Tarnley was talking fluently in an undertone.
Then came a silence, during which the old
Dutch clock struck one.

Lilly Dogger's eyes were wide open now,
and her ears erect. She heard no one an-

swer the old woman, who resumed her talk
in a minute ; and now she seemed careful
to make no avoidable noise—speaking low,
and when she moved about the kitchen
treading softly, and moving anything she
had to stir gently. Altogether she was now
taking as much care not to disturb as she had
shown carelessness upon the subject before.

Lilly Dogger again slipped out of bed, and
peeped through the keyhole. But she could
not see Mrs. Tarnley nor her companion, if
she had one.

Old Mildred was talking on, not in her
grumbling interrupted soliloquy, but in the
equable style of one spinning a long narra-
tive. This hum was relieved now and then
by the gentle clink of a teacup, or the jingle
of a spoon.

If Mrs. Tarnley was drinking her tea alone
at this hour of night and talking so to
herself, she was doing that she had never
done before, thought the curious little girl ;
and she must be a-going mad. From this

latter apprehension, however, she was relieved by hearing some one cough. It was not Mrs. Tarnley, who suspended her story, however. But there was an unmistakable difference of tone in this cough, and old Mildred said more distinctly something about a cure for a cough which she recommended.

Then came an answer in an odd drawling voice. The words she could not hear, but there could no longer be any doubt as to the presence of a stranger in the kitchen.

Lilly Dogger was rather frightened, she did not quite know why, and listened without power to form a conjecture. It was plain that the person who enjoyed old Mildred's hospitality was not her master, nor her mistress, nor old Dulcibella Crane.

As she listened, and wondered, and speculated sleep overtook her once more, and she quite forgot the dialogue, and the kitchen, and Mildred Tarnley's tea, and went off upon her own adventures in the wild land of dreams.

CHAPTER III.

THE LADY HAS HER TEA.

"You suffers dreadful, ma'am," said Mildred Tarnley. "Do you have them toothaches still."

"'Twas not toothache—a worse thing," said the stranger, demurely, who, with closed eyes, and her hand propping her head, seemed to have composed herself for a doze in the great chair.

"Wuss than toothache! That's bad. Earache mayhap?" inquired Mrs. Tarnley with pathetic concern, though I don't think it would have troubled her much if her guest had tumbled over the precipice of Carwell Valley and broken her neck among the stones in the brook.

"Pain in my face—it is called tic," said

the lady, with closed eyes in a languid drawl.

"Tic? lawk! Well, I never heard o' the like, unless it be the field-bug as sticks in the cattle—that's a bad ailment, I do suppose," conjectured Mrs. Tarnley.

"You may have it yourself some day," said this lady, who spoke quietly and deliberately, but with fluency, although her accent was foreign. "When we are growing a little old our bones and nerves they will not be young still. You have your rheumatism, I have my tic—the pain in my cheek and mouth—a great deal worse, as you will find, whenever you taste of it, as it may happen. Your tea is good—after a journey tea is so refreshing. I cannot live without my cup of tea, though it is not good for my tic. So, ha, ha, he-ha! There is the tea already in my cheek—oh! Well, you will be so good to give me my bag."

Mildred looked about, and found a small baize bag with an umbrella and a bandbox.

"There's a green bag I have here, ma'am."

"A baize bag?"

"Yes, 'm."

"Give it to me. Ha, yes, my bibe—my bibe—and my box."

So this lady rummaged and extricated a pipe very like a meerschaum, and a small square box.

"Tibbacca!" exclaimed Mrs. Tarnley. The stranger interpreted the exclamation, without interrupting her preparations.

"Dobacco? no, better thing—some opium. You are afraid Mrs. Harry Fairfield, she would smell id. No—I do not wish to disturb her sleeb. I am quite private here, and do not wish to discover myself. Ya, ya, ya, hoo!"

It was another twinge.

"Sad thing, ma'am," said Mildred. "Better now, perhaps?"

"Put a stool under my feed. Zere, zere, sat will do. Now you light that match and

hold to the end of ze bibe, and I will zen be
bedder."

Accordingly Mildred Tarnley, strongly
tempted to mutter a criticism, but possibly
secretly in awe of the tall and "big-made"
woman who issued these orders, proceeded to
obey them.

" No great odds of a smell arter all," said
Mrs. Tarnley approvingly, after a little pause.

" And how long siuce Harry married ?"
inquired the smoker after another silence.

" I can't know that nohow ; but 'tis since
Master Charles gave 'em the lend o' the
house."

" Deeb people these Vairvields are,"
laughed the big woman drowsily.

" When will he come here ? "

" To-morrow or next day, I wouldn't wonder ; but he never stays long, and he comes
and goes as secret-like as a man about
a murder a'most."

" Ha, I dare say. Old Vairvield would
cut him over the big shoulders with his

horsewhip, I think. And when will your
master come ?"

"Master comes very seldom. Oh! ve-ry.
Just when he thinks to find Master Henry
here, maybe once in a season."

"And where does he live—at home or
where ?" asked the tall visitor.

"Well, I can't say, I'm sure, if it baint at
Wyvern. At Wyvern, I do suppose, mostly.
But I daresay he travels a bit now and again.
I don't know I'm sure."

"Because I wrote to him to Wyvern to
meet me here. Is he at Wyvern ?"

"Well, faith, I can't tell. I know no more
than you, ma'am, where Master Charles is,"
said Mildred, with energy, relieved in the
midst of her rosary of lies to find herself free
to utter one undoubted truth.

"You have been a long time in the family,
Mrs. Tarnley ?" drawled the visitor, listlessly.

"Since I was the height o' that—before I
can remember. I was born in Carwell gate-

house here.   My mother was here in old
Squire's time, meanin' the father o' the present Harry Fairfield o' Wyvern that is, and
grandfather o' the two young gentlemen,
Master Charles and Master Harry.   Why,
bless you, my grandfather, that is my
mother's father, was in charge o' the house
and farm, and the woods, and the tenants,
and all ; there wasn't a tree felled, nor a
cow sold, nor an acre o' ground took up but
jest as he said.   They called him honest Tom
Pennecuick ; he was thought a great deal
of, my grandfather was, and Carwell never
turned in as good a penny to the Fairfields
as in his time ; not since, and not before—
never, and never will, that's sure."

"And which do you like best, Squire
Charles or Squire Harry ? " inquired the
languid lady.

"I likes Charles," said Mrs. Tarnley, with
decision.

"And why so ?"

"Well, Harry's a screw ; ye see he'd as

lief gie a joint o' his thumb as a sixpence. He'll take his turn out of every one good-humoured enough, and pay for trouble wi' a joke and a laugh ; a very pleasant gentle-man for such as has nothing to do but exchange work for his banter and live with-out wages ; all very fine. I never seed a shillin' of hisn since he had one to spend."

"Mr. Charles can be close-fisted too, when he likes it ? " suggested the lady.

"No, no, no, he's not that sort if he had it. Open-handed enough, and more the gentle-man every way than Master Harry—more the gentleman," answered Mildred.

"Yes, Harry Fairfield is a shrewd, hard man, I believe ; he ought to have helped his brother a bit ; he has saved a nice bit o' money, I dare say," said the visitor.

"If he hasn't a good handful in his kist corner 't'aint that he wastes what he gets."

"I do suppose he'll pay his brother a fair rent for the house ?" said the visitor.

"Master Harry'll pay for no more than he can help," observed Mildred.

"It's a comfortable house," pursues the stranger; "'twas so when I was here."

"Warm and roomy," acquiesced Mrs. Tarnley—"chimbley, roof, and wall—staunch and stout; 'twill stand a hundred year to come, wi' a new shingle and a daub o' mortar now and again. There's a few jackdaws up in the chimbleys that ought to be drew out o' that wi' their sticks and dirt," she reflected, respectfully.

"And do you mean to tell me he pays no rent for the Grange, and keeps his wife here?" demanded the lady, peremptorily.

"I know nothing about their dealings," answered Mrs. Tarnley, as tartly.

"And 't'aint clear to me I should care much neither; they'll settle that, like other matters, without stoppin' to ask Mildred what she thinks o't; and I dare say Master Harry will be glad enough to take it for nothing, if Master Charles will be fool enough to let him."

"Well, he shan't do that, I'll take care," said the lady, maintaining her immovable pose, which, with a certain peculiarity in the tone of her voice, gave to her an indescribable and unpleasant langour.

"I never have two pounds to lay on top o' one another. Jarity begins at home. I'll not starve for Master Harry," and she laughed softly and unpleasantly.

"His wife, you say, is a starved gurate's daughter!"

"Parson Maybell—poor he was, down at Wyvern Vicarage—meat only twice or thrice a week, as I have heard say, and treated old Squire Harry bad, I hear, about his rent; and old Squire Fairfield was kind—to *her* anyhow, and took her up to the hall, and so when she grew up she took her opportunity and married Master Harry."

"She was clever to catch such a shrewd chap—clever. Light again; I shall have

three four other puff before I go to my bed—
very clever. How did she take so well, and
hold so fast, that wise fellow, Harry Fairfield ?"

" Hoo ! fancy, I do suppose, and liken'.
She's a pretty lass. All them Fairfields
married for beauty mostly. Some o' them
got land and money, and the like, but a
pretty face allays along with the fortune."

The blind stranger, for blind she was,
smiled downward, faintly and slily, while she
was again preparing the pipe.

" When will Harry come again ?" she
asked.

" I never knows, he's so wary ; do you
want to talk to him, ma'am ?" said Mildred.

" Yes, I do," said she ; " hold the match
now, Mrs. Tarnley, please."

So she did, and—puff, puff, puff—about a
dozen times, went the smoke, and the smoker
was satisfied.

" Well, I never knows the minute, but it

mightn't be for a fortnight," said Mrs. Tarnley.

"And when Mr. Charles Fairfield come?" asked the visitor.

"If he's got your letter he'll be here quick enough. If it's missed him he mayn't set foot in it for three months' time. That's how it is wi' him," answered Mildred.

"What news of old Harry at Wyvern?" asked the stranger.

"No news in partic'lar," answered Mildred, "only he's well and hearty—but that's no news; the Fairfields is a long-lived stock, as everyone knows; he'll not lie in oak and wool for many a day yet, I'm thinkin'."

Perhaps she had rightly guessed the object of the lady's solicitude, for a silence followed.

"There's a saying in my country—'God's children die young,'" said the tall lady.

"And here about they do say, the Devil takes care of his own," said Mildred Tarnley. "But see how my score o' years be runnin' up, I take it sinners' lives be lengthened out a bit by the Judge of all, to gi'e us time to stay our thoughts a little, and repent our misdeeds, while yet we may."

"You have made a little fire in my room, Mrs. Tarnley?" inquired the stranger, who had probably no liking for theology.

"Yes 'm; everything snug."

"Would you mind running up and looking? I detest a chill," said this selfish person.

At that hour no doubt Mrs. Tarnley resented this tax on her rheumatics; but though she was not a woman to curb her resentments she made shift on this occasion; that did not prevent her, however, from giving the stranger a furious look, while she muttered inaudibly a few words.

"I'll go with pleasure, ma'am, but I'm sure it's all right," she said aloud, very civilly, and paused, thinking perhaps that the lady would would let her off the long walk upstairs to the front of the house.

" Very good; I'll wait here," said the guest, unfeelingly.

" As you please'm," said Mildred, and with a parting look round the kitchen, she took the candle, and left the lady to the light of the fire.

The lady was almost reclining in her chair, as if she were dozing; but in a few moments up she stood, and placing her hand by her ear, listened; then, with her hands advanced, she crept slowly, and as noiselessly as a cat, across the floor. She jostled a little against the table at Lilly Dogger's door; then she stopped perfectly still, withdrew the table without a sound; the door swung a little open, and the gaunt figure in grey stood at it, listening. A very faint flicker from the fire lighted this dim woman, who seemed for the moment to have no more life in her than the tall, gray stone of the Druid's hoe on Cressley Common.

Lilly Dogger was fast asleep; but broken were her slumbers destined to be that night. She felt a hand on her neck, and looking up, could not for a while see anything, so dark was the room.

She jumped up in a sitting posture, with a short cry of fear, thinking that she was in the hands of a robber.

"*Be* quiet, fool," said the tall woman, slipping her hand over the girl's mouth. "I'm a lady, a friend of Mrs. Mildred Tarnley, and I'm gome to stay in the house. Who is the lady that sleeps upstairs in the room that used to be Mr. Harry's? You must answer true, or I'll pull your ear very hard."

"It is the mistress, please 'm," answered the frightened girl.

"Married lady?"

"Yes 'm."

"Who is her husband?"

With this question the big fingers of her visitor closed upon Lilly Dogger's ear with a monitory pinch.

"The master, ma'am."

" And what's the master's name, you dirdy liddle brevarigator?"

And with these words her ear was wrung sharply.

She would have cried, very likely, if she had been less frightened, but she only winced, with her shoulders up to her ears, and answered in tremulous haste—

" Mr. Fairfield, sure."

" There's three Mr. Vairvields : there's old Mr. Vairvield, there's Mr. Charles Vairvield, and there's Mr. Harry Vairvield—you *shall* speak plain."

And at each name in her catalogue she twisted the child's ear with a sharp separate wring.

" Oh, law, ma'am. Please'm, I mean Mr. Charles Fairfield. I didn't mean to tell you no story, indeed, my lady."

" Ho, ho—yes — Charles, Charles — very goot. Now, you tell me how you know Mr. Harry from Mr. Charles ?" ·

" Oh, law, ma'am ! oh, law ! oh, ma'am, dear ! sure, you won't pull it no more, good lady, pleas—my ear's most broke," gasped the girl, who felt the torture beginning again.

"You tell truth. How do you know Mr. Charles from Mr. Harry?"

"Mr. Charles has bigger eyes, ma'am, and Mr. Harry has lighter hair, and a red face, please'm, and Mr. Charles's face is brown, and he talks very quiet-like, and Mr. Harry talks very loud, and he's always travellin' about a-horseback, and Mr. Charles is the eldest son, and the little child they're lookin' for is to be the Squire o' Wyvern."

The interrogator here gave her a hard pinch by the ear, perhaps without thinking of it, for she said nothing for a minute nearly, and the girl remained with her head buried between her shoulders, and her eyes wide open, staring straight up where she conjectured her examiner's face might be.

"Is the man that talks loud—Mr. Harry— here often?" asked the voice at her bedside.

"But seldom, ma'am—too busy at fairs and races, I hear them say."

" And Mr. Charles—is he often here ? "

" Yes'm ; master be always here, exceptin'
this time only ; he's gone about a week."

" About a week, Mr. Charles ? "

" Oh la, ma'am—-yes, indeed, ma'am,
dear, it's just a week to-day since master
went."

Here was a silence.

" That will do. If I find you've been
telling me lies I'll take ye by the back of the
neck and squeeze your face against the
kitchen bars till it's burnt through and
through—do you see ; and I give you this
one. chance, if you have been telling lies to
say so, and I'll forgive you."

" Nothing but truth, indeed and indeed,
ma'am."

" Old Tarnley will beat you if she hears
you have told me anything. So keep your
own secret, and I'll not tell of you."

She saw the brawny outline of the woman
faintly like a black shadow as she made her
way through the door, into the kitchen, and

she heard the door close, and the table shoved cautiously back into its place, and then, with a beating heart, she lay still and awfully wide-awake in the dark.

CHAPTER IV.

THROUGH THE HOUSE.

THIS stalwart lady stumbled and groped her way back to her chair, and sat down again in the kitchen. The chair in which she sat was an old-fashioned arm-chair of plain wood, uncoloured and clumsy.

When Mildred Tarnley returned the changed appearance of her guest struck her.

"Be ye sick, ma'am?" she asked, standing, candle in hand, by the chair.

The visitor was sitting bolt upright, with a large hand clutched on each arm of the chair, with a face deadly pale and distorted by a frown or a spasm that frightened old Mildred, who fancied, as she made no sign, not the slightest stir, that she was in a fit, or possibly dead.

"For God's sake, ma'am," conjured old Mildred, fiercely, "*will* ye speak?"

The lady in the chair started, shrugged, and gasped. It was like shaking off a fit.

"Ho! oh, Mildred Tarnley, I was thinking —I was thinking—did you speak?"

Mildred looked at her, not knowing what to make of it. Too much laudanum—was it? or that nervous pain in her head.

"I only asked you how you were, ma'am— you looked so bad. I thought you was just going to work in a fit."

"What an old fool! I never was better in my life—*fit!* I never had a fit—not I."

"You used to have 'em sometimes, long ago, ma'am, and they came in the snap of a finger, like," said Mildred, sturdily.

"Clear your head of those fits, for they have left me long ago. I'm well, I tell you —never was better. You're old—you're old, woman, and that which has made you so pious is also making you blind."

"Well, you look a deal better now—you

do," said Mildred, who did not want to have a corpse or an epileptic suddenly on her hands, and was much relieved by the signs of returning vivacity and colour.

" Tarnley, you've been a faithful creature and true to me ; I hope I may live to reward you," said the lady, extending her hand vaguely towards the old servant.

" I'm true to them as gives me bread, and ever was, and that's old Mildred Tarnley's truth. If she eats their bread, she'll maintain their right, and that's only honest—that's reason, ma'am."

" I have no right to cry no ; I cry excellent, good, good, very good, for as you are my husband's servant, I have all the benefit of your admirable fidelity. Boo! I am so grateful, and one day or other, old girl, I'll reward you—and very good tea, and every care of me. I will tell Mr. Vairvield when he comes how good you have been—and, tell me, how is the fire, and the bed, and the bedroom—all quite comfortable ? "

"Comfortable, quite, I hope, ma'am."

"Do I look quite well now?"

"Yes'm, pure and hearty. It was only just a turn."

"Yes, just so, perhaps, although I never felt it, and I could dance now only for—fifty things, so I won't mind." She laughed. "I'm sleepy, and I'm *not* sleepy; and I love you, old Mildred Tarnley, and you'll tell me some more about Master Harry and his wife when we get upstairs. Who'd have thought that wild fellow would ever tie himself to a wife? Who'd have fancied that clever young man that loves making money so well, would have chosen out a wife without a florin to her fortune? Everything is so surprising. Come, let's have a laugh, you and me together."

"My laughing days is over, ma'am—not that I see much to laugh at for any one, and many a thing I thought a laughing matter when I was young seems o'erlike a crying matter now I'm grown old," said old Mildred, and snuffed the kitchen candle with her fingers.

"Well, give me your arm, Mildred; there's a good old thing—yes."

And up she got her long length. Mildred took the candle and took the tall lady gently by the wrist. The guest, however, placed her great hand upon Mildred's shoulder, and thus they proceeded through the passages. Leaving the back stair that led to Alice's room, at the right, they mounted the great staircase and reached a comfortably warm room with a fire flickering on the hearth, for the air was sharp. In other respects the apartment had not very much to boast.

"There's fire here, I feel it; place my chair near it. The bed in the old place?" said the tall woman, coming to a halt.

"Yes'm. Little change here, ever, I warrant ye, only the room's bin new papered," answered Mildred.

"New papered, has it? Well, I'll sit down—thanks—and I'll get to my bed, just now."

"Shall I assist ye, ma'am?"

" By-and-by, thanks ; but not till I have eaten a bit. I have grown hungry, what your master calls peckish. What do you advise ? "

" I would advise your eating something," replied Mildred.

" But what ? "

" There's very little ; there's eggs quite new, there's a bit o' bacon, and there's about half a cold chicken—roast, and there's a corner o' Chedder cheese, and there's butter, and there's bread—'taint much," answered Mrs. Tarnley, glibly.

" The chicken will do very nicely, and don't forget bread and salt, Mrs. Tarnley, and a glass of beer."

" Yes'm."

Mrs. Tarnley poked the fire and looked about her, and then took the only candle, marched boldly off with it, shutting the door.

Toward the door the lady turned her face and listened. She heard old Mildred's step receding.

This tall woman was not pleasant to look at. Her large features were pitted with the small-pox and deadly pale with the pallor of anger, and an unpleasant smile lighted up the whiteness of her face.

"Patience, patience," she repeated, "what a d——d trick! no matter, wait a little."

She did wait a little in silence, screwing her lips and knitting her brows, and then a new resource struck her, and she groped in her bag and drew forth a bottle, which she applied to her lips more than once, and seemed better. It was no febrifuge nor opiate; but though the flicker of the fire showed no flush on her pallid features, the odour declared it brandy.

CHAPTER V.

THE BELL RINGS.

" WILL that beast never go to bed—even there, I mind, she used to sleep with an eye open and an ear cocked—and nowhere safe from her never—here and there, up and down, without a stir or a breath, like a ghost or a devil?"—thought Mrs. Tarnley. " Thank God, she's blind now, that will quiet her."

Mildred was afraid of that woman. It was not only that she was cold and hard, but she was so awfully violent and wicked.

"Satan's her name. Lord help us, in what hell did he pick her up?" Mildred would say to herself, in old times, as with the important fury of fear, she used to knock about the kitchen utensils, and deal violently with every chair, table, spoon, or " cannikin " that came in her way.

The woman had fits, and bad fits too, in old times, when she knew her well.

" And she drank like a fish cogniac neat— and she was alive still, and millions of people, younger and better, that never had a fit, and kept their bodies in soberness and temperance, was gone dead and buried since ; and that drunken, shattered, battered creature, wi' her fallin' sickness and her sins and her years, was here alive and strong to plague and frighten better folk. Well, she's 'ad small-pox, thank God, and well mauled she is, and them spyin', glarin' eyes o' hers, the wild beast."

By this time Mrs. Tarnley was again in the kitchen. She did not take down the fire yet. She did not know, for certain, whether Charles Fairfield might not arrive. The London mail that passed by the town of Darwynd, beyond Cressley Common, came later than that divergent stage coach that changed

on the line of road that passes the Pied
Horse.

What a situation it would have been if
Charles Fairfield and the Vrau had found
themselves *vis-à-vis* as inside passengers in
the coach that night. Would the matter have
been much mended if the Dutch woman had
loitered long enough in the kitchen for Charles
to step in and surprise her? It was a thought
that occurred more than once to Mildred with
a qualm of panic. But she was afraid to
hasten the stranger's departure to her room,
for that lady's mind swarmed with suspicion
which a stir would set in motion.

" The Lord gave us dominion over the beast
o' the field, Parson Winyard said in his sermon
last Sunday; but we ain't allowed to kill nor
hurt, but for food or for defence ; and good
old Parson Buckles, that was as good as two
of he, said, I mind, the very same words. I
often thought o' them of late—merciful to
them brutes, for they was made by the one
Creator as made ourselves. So the merci-

ful man is merciful to his beast — will ye ? "

Mrs. Tarnley interrupted herself sharply, dealing on the lean ribs of the cat, who had got its head into a saucepan, a thump with a wooden spoon, which emitted a hollow sound and doubled the thief into a curve.

" Merciful, of course, except when they're arter mischief ; but them that's noxious, and hurtful, and dangerous, we're free to kill ; and where's the beast so dangerous as a real bad man or woman ? God forbid I should do wrong. I'm an old woman, nigh-hand the grave, and murder's murder !—I do suppose and allow that's it. Thou shalt do no murder. No more I would—no, not if an angel said do it ; no, I wouldn't for untold goold. But I often wondered why if ye may, wi' a good conscience, knock a snake on the head wi' a stone, and chop a shovel down smack on a toad, ye should stay your hand, and let a devil incarnate go her murdering way through the world, blastin' that one wi' lies, robbin' this one wi' craft, and murderin' t'other, if it make for her interest, wi' poison or perjury. Lord help my poor head, and forgive me if it be sin, but I can find neither right nor reason in that, nor see, nohow, why she shouldn't be killed off-hand like a rat or a sarpent."

At this point the bell rang loud and sudden, and Mrs. Tarnley bounced and blessed herself. There was no great difficulty in settling from what quarter the summons came, for, except the hall door bell, which was a deep-toned sonorous one, there was but one in the house in ringing order, and that was of the bed-room where her young mistress lay.

" Well, here's a go! Who'd a' thought o' her awake at these hours, and out o' her bed, and a pluckin' at her bell. I doubt it *is* her. The like was never before. 'Tis enough to frighten a body. The Lord help us."

Mrs. Tarnley stood straight as a grenadier on drill with her back to the fire, the poker with which, during her homily, she had been raking the bars, still in her hand.

" This night 'ill be the death o' me. Everything's gone cross and contrary. Here's that
young silly lass awake and out o' her bed, that
never had an eye open at these hours, since
she came to the Grange, before ; and there's
that other one in the state-room, not that
far from her, as wide awake as she ; and
here's Master Charles a comin', mayhap, this
minute wi' his drummin' and bellin' at the
hall door. 'Tis enough to make a body
swear; 't has given me the narves and
the tremblins, and I don't know how it's
to end."

And Mrs. Tarnley unconsciously shouldered
her poker as if awaiting the assault of burg-
lars, and vaguely thought if Charles arrived
as she had described, what power on earth
could keep the peace ?

Again the bell rang.

" Well, *there's* patience for ye ! "

She halted at the kitchen door, with the
candle in her hand, listening, with a stern,
frightened face. She was thinking whether

Alice might not have been frightened by some fantastic terror in her room.

"She has that old fat fool, Dulcibella Crane, only a room off—why don't she call up her?"

But Mrs. Tarnley at length did go on, and up the stairs, and heard Alice's voice call along the passage, in a loud tone,—

"Mrs. Tarnley! is that *you*, Mrs. Tarnley?"

"Me, ma'am? Yes'm. I thought I heard your bell ring, and I had scant time to hustle my clothes on. Is there anything uncommon a-happenin', ma'am, or what's expected just now from an old woman like me?"

"Oh, Mrs. Tarnley, I beg your pardon, I'm so sorry, and I would not disturb you, only that I heard a noise, and I thought Mr. Charles might have arrived."

"No, ma'am, he's not come, nor no sign o' him. You told me, ma'am, his letter said there was but small chance o't."

"So I did, Mildred—so it did. Still a

chance—just a chance—and I thought, perhaps——"

"There's no perhaps in it, ma'am; he baint
come."

"Dulcibella tells me she thought some time
ago she heard some one arrive."

"So she did, mayhap, for there did come a
message for Master Harry from the farmer
beyond Gryce's mill; but he went his way
again."

Mildred was fibbing with a fluency that
almost surprised herself.

"I dessay you've done wi' me now, ma'am?"
said Mildred. "Lugged out o' my bed, ma'am,
at these hours—my achin' old bones—'taint
what I'm used to, asking your pardon for
making so free."

"I'm really very sorry—you won't be vexed
with me. Good night, Mildred."

"Your servant, ma'am."

And Mrs. Tarnley withdrew from the door
where Alice stood before her with her dressing-
gown about her shoulders, looking so pale and

deprecatory and anxious, that I wonder even Mildred Tarnley did not pity her.

" I'm tellin' lies enough to break a bridge, and me that's vowed against lying so stiff and strong over again only Monday last."

She shook her head slowly, and with a sudden qualm of conscience.

" Well, in for a penny in for a pound. It's only for to-night; mayhap, and I can't help it, and if that old witch was once over the door-stone I'd speak truth the rest o' my days, as I ha' done, by the grace o' God, for more than a month, and here's a nice merry-go-round for my poor old head. Who's to keep all straight and smooth wi' them that's in the house, and, mayhap comin'? And that ghost upstairs,—she'll be gropin' and screechin' through the house, and then there'll be the devil to pay wi' her and the poor lass up there—if I don't gi'e her her supper quick. Come, bustle, bustle, be alive," she muttered, as this thought struck her with new force; and so to the little " safe " which served that

miniature household for larder she repaired.
Plates clattered, and knives and forks, and
the dishes in the safe slid forth, and how near
she was forgetting the salt! and "the bread,
all right," so here was a tray very comfortably
furnished, and setting the candlestick upon it
also, she contemplated the supper, with a fierce
sneer, and a wag of her head.

"How sick and weak we be! Tea and
toast and eggs down here, and this little bit
in her bed-room—heaven bless her—la' love
it, poor little darling, don't I hope it may do
her good?—I wish the first mouthful may
choke her—keeping me on the trot to these
hours, old beast."

Passing the stairs, Mrs. Tarnley crept softly,
and took pains to prevent her burden from
rattling on the tray, while there rose in her
brain the furious reflection,—

"Pretty rubbish that I should be this way
among 'em!"

And she would have liked to dash the tray
on the floor at the foot of the stairs, and to

leave the startled inhabitants to their own courses.

This, of course, was but an emotion. The old woman completed her long march cautiously, and knocked at the *Vrau's* door.

"Come in, dear," said the inmate, and Mildred Tarnley, with her tray in her hands, marched into the room, and looked round peevishly for a table to set it down on.

"You'll find all as you said, 'm," said old Tarnley. "Shall I set it before you, or will you move this way, please 'm?"

"Before me, dear."

So Mildred carried the table and supper over, and placed it before the lady, who sat up and said,—

"Good Mildred, how good you are; give me now the knife and fork, in my fingers, and put some salt just there. Very good. How good of you to take so much trouble for poor me, you kind old Mildred?"

How wondrous sweet she had grown in a minute. The old servant, who knew her, was not conciliated, but disgusted, and looked hard at the benevolent lady, wondering what could be in her mind.

"If everything's right, I'll wish you good night, 'm, and I'll go down to my bed, ma'am, please."

"Wait a while with me. Do, there's a good soul. I'll not detain you long, you dear old lass."

"Well, ma'am, I must go down and take down the fire, and shut-to the door, or the rats will be in from the scullery; and I'll come up again, ma'am, in a few minutes."

And not waiting for permission, Mildred Tarnley, who had an anxiety of another sort in her head, took the candle in her hand and left the guest at her supper by the light of the fire.

She shut the door quickly lest her departure should be countermanded, and trotted away and downstairs, but not to the kitchen.

CHAPTER VI.

TOM IS ORDERED UP.

WHEN she reached the foot of the stairs that leads to the gallery on which the room occupied by Alice opens, instead of pursuing her way to the kitchen she turned into a narrow and dark passage that is hemmed in on the side opposite to the wall by the ascending staircase.

The shadows of the banisters on the panelled oak flew after one another in sudden chase as the old woman glided by, and looking up and back she stopped at the door of a small room, constructed as we see in similar old houses, under the stairs. On the panel of this she struck a muffled summons with her fist, and on the third or fourth the startled voice of Tom demanded roughly from within,—

" *What*'s that ? "

" Hish ! " said the old woman, through a bit of the open door.

" 'Tis Mrs. Tarnley—only me."

" Lauk, woman, ye did take a rise out o' me. I thought ye was—I don't know what —I was a dreaming, I think."

" Never mind, you must be awake for an hour or so," said Mrs. Tarnley, entering the den without more ceremony.

Tom didn't mind Mrs. Tarnley, nor Mrs. Tarnley Tom, a rush. She set the candle on the tiled floor. Tom was sitting in his shirt on the side of his " settlebed," with his hands on his knees.

" Ye must get on your things, Tom, and if ever you stirred yourself, be alive now. The master's a comin', and may be here, across Cressley Common in half an hour, or might be in five minutes, and ye must go out a bit and meet him, and—are ye awake ? "

" Starin'. Go on."

" Ye'll tell him just this, the big woman as lives at Hoxton——"

" Hoxton ! *Well ?*"

" That Master Harry has all the trouble wi', has come here, angry, in search of Master Harry, mind, and is in the bedroom over the hall-door. Will ye mind all that now ? "

" Ay," said Tom, and repeated it.

" Well, he'll know better whether it's best for him to come on or turn back. But if come on he will, let him come in at the kitchen door, mind, and you go that way, too, and he'll find neither bolt nor bar, but open doors, and nothing but the latch between him and the kitchen, and me sitting by the fire ; but don't you clap a door, nor tread heavy, but remember there's a sharp pair of ears that 'id hear a cricket through the three walls o' Carwell Grange."

She took up the candle, and herself listened for a moment at the door, and again turned her earnest and sinister face on Tom.

"And again, I say, Tom, if ever ye was quick, be quick now," and she clapped her lean hand down on his shoulder with a sort of fierce shake ; "and if ever ye trod soft, go softly now, *mind*."

Tom, who was scratching his head, and staring in her face, nodded.

"And mind you, the kitchen way, and afraid o' slips, say ye the message over again to me"

This he did, glibly enough.

"Here, light your candle from this, and if ye fail your master now, never call yourself man again.."

Having thus charged him, she went softly from this nook with its slanting roof, and thinking of the thankless world, and all the trouble her old bones and brain were put to, she lost her temper, at the foot of the great staircase, and was near turning back again to the kitchen, or perhaps whisking out of the door herself, and marching off to Cressley Common to meet her master, and shock and scare him all she could, and place her resignation, as more distinguished functionaries sometimes do theirs, in the hands of her employer, to prove his helplessness and her own importance, and so assert herself for time past and to come.

Her interview with Tom had not occupied much time. She knocked at the Vrau's door, and entering, found that person at the close of a greedy repast.

Emotions of fear, I suppose, disturb the appetite, much more than others. Not caring one farthing about Charles, she did not grieve at his infidelity ; taking profligacy for granted as the rule of life, it did not even shock her. But she was stung with a furious pang of jealousy, for that needs no love, being in its essence the sense of property invaded, supremacy insulted, and self despised. In this sort of jealousy there is neither the sublimity of despair nor the pathos of sorrow, but simply the malice, fury, and revenge of outraged egotism.

There she sat, unconscious of the glimmer of the firelight, feeding as a beast will bleeding after a blow. Beast she was, with the bestial faculty of cherishing a long revenge, with bestial treachery and seeming unconcern.

"Ho oh! you've come back," she cried, with playful reproach, "cruel old girl! you leave your poor vrau alone, alone among the ghosts—now, sit down, are you sitting? and tell me everything, and all the news—did you bring a little brandy or what?"

Her open hand was extended, and gently moving over the tray at about the level of the top of a bottle.

"No, ma'am, I haven't none in my charge, but there's a smell o' brandy about," said Mildred, who liked saying a disagreeable thing.

"So there ought," said the gaunt woman placidly, and lifted a big black bottle that lay in her lap, like a baby, folded in a grey shawl. "But I'll want this, don't you see, when I'm on my rambles again—get a little, there's a good girl, or if you can't get that, there's rum or gin, there never was a country-house without something in it; you know very well where Harry Vairvield is there will be liquor—I know him well."

"But he baint here now, as is well known to you, ma'am," said Mildred, dryly.

"I'm not going to waste my drink, while I think there's drink in the house. Who has a right before me, old girl?" said the stranger, grimly.

"Tut, ma'am, 'tis childish talkin' so, there's none in my charge, never a drop. Master Harry, I dare say, has summat under lock and key, but not me, and why should I tell you a lie about the like?"

"You never tell lies, old Mildred, I forgot that—but young as she is, I lay my life the woman, Mrs. Harry Vairvield, upstairs, likes a nip now and then, hey? and she has a boddle, I'll be bound, in her wardrobe, or if she's shy, 'twixt her bed and her mattress, ole rogue! you know very well, I think, does she? and if she likes it she sleeps sound, and go you, and while she snores, borrow you the bottle."

"She's nothing of the sort, she drinks nothing nowhere, much less in her bed-room, she's a perfect lady," said Mrs. Tarnley, in no mood to flatter her companion.

"Oh ho! that's so like old Mildred Tarnley! Dear old cat, I'm so amused, I could stroke her thin ribs, and pet her for making me laugh so by her frisks and capers instead of throwing you by the neck out of the window for scratching and spitting—I'm so good-natured. Do you tell lies, Mildred?"

"I 'a told a shameful lot in my day, ma'am, but not more mayhap than many a one that hasn't grace to say so."

"You read your Bible, Mildred," said the lady, who with a knife and fork was securing on her plate the morsels to which old Mildred helped her.

"Ay, ma'am, a bit now, and a bit again, never too late to repent, ma'am."

"Repentance and grace, you'll do, Mrs. Tarnley. It's a pleasure to hear you," said the lady, with her mouth rather full; "and you never see my husband?"

"Now and again, now and again, once and away he looks in."

"Never stays a week or a month at a time?"

"Week or a month!" echoed Mrs. Tarnley, looking quickly in the serene face of the lady, and then laughing off the suggestion scornfully. "You're thinking of old times, ma'am.

"Thinking, thinking, I don't think I was thinking at all," said the lady, answering Mildred's laugh with one more careless; "old times when he had a wife here, eh? old times! How old are they? Eh—that's eighteen years ago—you hardly knew me when I called here?"

"There was a change surely. I'd like to know who wouldn't in eighteen years, there's a change in me since then."

"I shouldn't wonder," said the lady, quietly. "Did he ever tell you how we quarreled?"

"Not he," answered Mildred.

"He's very close," said the stranger.

"A deal closer than Mr. Harry," acquiesced Mildred.

"Not like you and me, Mrs. Tarnley, that can't keep a secret—*never*. That tell truth, and shame the devil. I, because I don't care a snap of my fingers for you, or him, or the Archbishop of Canterbury; and you, because you're all for grace and repentance. How am I looking to-night—tired?"

"Tired, to be sure; you ought to be in your bed, ma'am, an hour ago; you're as white as that plate, ma'am."

"White are they?—so they used to be long ago," said the visitor.

"The same set, ma'am. 'Twas a long set

in my mother's time, though 'tis little better than a short set now ; but I don't think there's more than three plates, and the cracked butter-boat, that had a stitch in it. You'll mind, although ye may 'a forgot, for I usen't to send it up to table—only them three, and the butter-boat broke since ; and that butter-boat, 'twouldn't a brought three ha'pence by auction, and 'twas that little slut downstairs, that doesn't never do nothing right, that knocked it off the shelf, with her smashing."

"And I'm not looking well to-night ? " said this pallid woman.

" You'd be the better of a little blood to your cheeks ; you're as white as paper, ma'am," answered Mildred.

" I never *have* any colour now, they tell me—always pale, pale, pale ; but it isn't muddy ; 'taint what you call *putty ?* "

" Well, no."

" Ha ! no ; I knew that—*no*, and I'd rather be a little pale. I don't like your

great, coarse peony-faced women; it's seven
years in May last since I lost my sight.
Some people are persecuted; one curse after
another—rank injustice! Why should *I* lose
my sight, that never did anything to signify—
not half what others have, who enjoy health,
wealth, rank—everything. Things are topsy-
turvey a bit just now, but we'll see them
righted yet."

CHAPTER VII.

THE OLD SOLDIER GROWS MORE FRIENDLY, AND FRIGHTENS MRS. TARNLEY.

THE " Dutchwoman " resumed in a minute, and observed,—

" Well, old Tarnley, there's no good in talking where you can't right yourself, and where you can revenge, there's no good in talk either ; but gone it is, and the doctors say no cutting, nothing safe in my case ; no cure, so let it be. I liked dress once ; I dressed pretty well."

" Beautiful ! " exclaimed old Mildred, kindling for a moment into her earlier admiration of the French and London finery, with which once this tall and faded beauty had amazed the solitudes of Carwell.

The bleached, big woman smiled—almost laughed with gratified vanity.

"Yes, I was well dressed—something better than the young dowdies and old fromps, in this part of the world. How I used to laugh at them! I went to church, and to the races, to see them. Well, we'll have better times yet at Wyvern; the old man there can't live for ever; he's not the Wandering Jew, and he can't be far from a hundred; and so sure as Charles is my husband, I'll have you there, if you like it, or give you a snug house, and a bit of ground, and a garden, and a snug allowance monthly, if you like this place best. I love my own, and you've been true to me, and I never failed a friend."

"I'm growing old and silly, ma'am—never so strong as I was took for. The will was ever stronger with Mildred than the body, bless ye—no, no; two or three quiet years to live as I should a lived always, wi' an eye on my Bible and an eye on my ways—not that I ever did aught I need be one bit ashamed on—no, not I ; honest and sober, and most respectable, thank God, as the family will testify, and the neighbours ; but I'll not deny, 'twould be something not that bad, if my old bones could rest a bit," said old Mildred.

"Ha, girl, they *shall;* your old bones shall rest, my child," said the lady.

"They'll rest some day in the old churchyard o' Carwell, but not much sooner, I'm thinking," said Mrs. Tarnley.

"Folly, folly ! ole girl ; you've many a year to go before that journey ; you'll live to see me, Mrs. Vairvield of Wyvern, and it won't be a bad day for you, old Mildred."

The "Dutchwoman," or the old soldier, as they used to call her long ago in this sequestered nook, drawled this languidly, and yawned a long, listless yawn.

"Well, ma'am, if you're tired, so am I," said Mildred, a little tartly ; "and as for dreamin' o' quiet in this world, I ha' cleared

my head o' that nonsense many a year ago.
There's little good can happen old Mildred
now, and less I look for, and none I'll seek,
ma'am ; and as for a roof over my head for
nothing, and that bit o' ground ye spoke of,
and wages to live on without no work, I don't
believe there's no such luck going for no
one."

"Listen to me, Mildred," said the stranger,
more sternly than before; "is it because I
don't swear you won't believe ? Hear, now,
once for all, and understand : I'll make *that*
a good day for you that makes me the lady
of Wyvern. Sharp and hard I've been with
those I owed a knock to, but I never yet
forgot a friend ; you may do me a service
to-morrow or next day, *mind,* and if you
stand by me, I'll stand by you ; you need
but ask and have, ask what you *will.*"

"Well, now, ma'am—bah ! what talk it is !
Lawk, ma'am ; don't I know the world,
ma'am, and what sort o' place it is ? I a'
bin promised many a fine thing in my day,

and here I am still—old and weary—among
the pots and pans every night and mornin',
and up to my elbows in suds every Saturday;
that's all that ever came o' fine promises to
Mildred Tarnley."

" Well, you used to say, it's a long lane
that has no turn. You'll have a glass of
this ? " and she popped the brandy-bottle on
the table beside her, with her hand fast
on its neck.

" No brandy—no nothing, ma'am, I. thank
ye."

" What ! no brandy ?   Pish, girl, nonsense."

" No, ma'am, I thank ye, I never drinks
nothing o' the sort—a mug o' beer after
washing or the like—but my headache never
would abear brandy."

" Once and away—come," solicited the old
soldier.

" No, I thank ye, ma'am ; I'll swallow
nothing o' the kind, please."

" What a mule ! You won't have a nip

with an old friend, after so long an absence
—come, Mildred, come ; where's the glass ? "

"Here's the glass, 'm, but not a drop for
me, ma'am ; I won't drink nothing o' the
sort, please."

"Not from me, I suppose ; but if you
mean to say you never do, I don't believe
you," said the Dutchwoman, more nettled, it
seemed, than such a failure of good fellowship
in Mrs. Tarnley would naturally have war-
ranted. Perhaps she had particularly strong
reasons for making old Mildred frank, genial,
and intimate that night.

"I don't tell lies," said Mildred.

"Don't you ? " said the " old soldier," and
elevated the brows of her sightless eyes,
and screwed her lips with ugly ridicule.

Mrs. Tarnley looked with a dark shrewd-
ness upon this meaning mask, trying to discover the exact force of its significance. She
felt very uncomfortable.

The blind woman's face expanded into a
broad smile. She shrugged, shook her head,

and laughed. How odiously wide her face looked as she laughed ! Mildred did not know exactly what to make of her.

" But if you did tell lies," drawled the lady, " even to me, what does it matter, if you promised to tell no more ?' So let us shake hands—where's your hand ? "

And she kept shuffling her big hand upon the table, palm upward, with its fingers groping in the air like the claws of a crab upon its back.

" Give me—give me—give me your hand, I say," said she.

"'Tain't for the like o' me," replied Mildred, with grim formality.

" You'd better be friendly. Come, give me your hand."

" Well, ma'am, 'tain't for me to dispute your pleasure," answered the old servant, and she slipped her hard fingers upon the upturned palm of the Dutchwoman, who clutched them with a strenuous friendship, and held them fast.

"I like you, Tarnley; we've had rough words, sometimes, but no ill blood, and I'll do what I said. I never failed a friend, as you will see, if only you *be* my friend; and why or for whom should you *not?* Tut, we're not fools!"

"The time is past for me to quarrel, being to the wrong side o' sixty more than you'd suppose, and quiet all I wants — quiet, ma'am."

"Yes, quiet and comfort, too, and both you shall have, Mildred Tarnley, if you don't choose to quarrel with those who *would* be kind to you, if you'd let them. Yes, indeed, who *would* be kind, and *very* kind, if you'd only let them. No, leave your hand where it is, I can't see you, and it's sometimes dull work talking only to a voice. If I can't see you I'll feel you, and hold you, old girl—hold you fast till I know what terms we're on."

All this time she had Mildred Tarnley's hand between hers, and was fondling and kneading it as a rustic lover in the agonies of the momentous question might have done fifty years ago.

"I don't know what you want me to say, ma'am, no more than the plate there. Little good left in Mildred Tarnley now, and small power to help or hurt anyone, great or small, at these years."

"I want you to be friendly with me, that's all; I ask no more, and it ain't a great deal, all things considered. Friendly talk, of course, ain't all I mean, that's civility, and civility's very well, very pleasant, like a lady's fan, or her lap-dog, but nothing at a real pinch, nothing to fight a wolf with. Come, old Mildred, Mildred Tarnley, good Mildred, can I be sure of you, *quite* sure?"

"Sure and certain, ma'am, in all honest service."

"Honest service! Yes, of course; what else could we think of? You used to like, I remember, Mildred, a nice ribbon in your bonnet. I have two pieces quite new. I brought them from London. Satin ribbon—

purple one is—I know you'll like it, and you'll drink a glass of this to please me."

"Thanks for the ribbons, ma'am, I'll not refuse 'em; but I won't drink nothing, ma'am, I thank you."

"Well, please yourself in that. Pour out a little for me, there's a glass, ain't there?"

"Yes, 'm. How much will you have, ma'am?"

"Half a glass. There's a dear. Stingy half glass," she continued, putting her finger in to gauge the quantity. "Go on, go on, remember my long journey to-day. Do you smoke, Mildred?"

"Smoke, 'm? No, 'm! Dear me, there's no smell o' tobacco, is there?" said Mildred, who was always suspecting Tom of smoking slily in his crib under the stairs.

"Smell, no; but I smoke a pinch of tobacco now and again myself, the doctor says I must, and a breath just of opium when I want it. You can have a pipe of tobacco

if you like, child, and you needn't be shy.
Well ? "

" Ho, Fau !   No, ma'am, I thank ye."

" Fau ! " echoed the Dutchwoman, with a
derisive, chilling laugh, which apprized old
Mildred of her solecism. But the lady did
not mean to quarrel.

" What sort of dress have you for Sundays,
going to church, and all that ? "

" An old dress it is now. I had the
material, ye'll mind, when ye was here, long
ago ; but it wasn't made up till long after.
It's very genteel, the folk all says. Chocolate
colour—British cashmere—'twas old Mrs.
Hartlepool, the parson's widow, made me a
compliment o't when she was goin', and I
kept it all the time, wi' whole pepper and
camphor, in my box, by my bed, and it
looked as fresh when I took it out to give it
to Miss Maddox to make up as if 'twas just
put new on the counter. She did open her
eyes, that's nigh seven years gone, when I
told her how old it was."

"Heyday! Hi! I think I do remember that old chocolate thing. Why, it can't be that, that's twenty years old. Well, look in my box, here's the key. You'll see two books with green leather backs and gold. Can ye read? I'm going to make you a present."

"I *can* read, ma'am; but I scarce have time to read my Bible."

"The Bible's a good book, but that's a better," said the lady, with one of her titters. "But it ain't a book I'm going to give you. Look it out, green and gold, there are only two in the box. It is the one that has an I and a V on the back, *four*, the fourth volume. I have little else to amuse me. I have the news of the neighbours, but I don't like 'em, who could? A bad lot, they hate one another; 'twouldn't be a worse world if they were all hanged. They hate me because I'm a lady, so I don't cry when baby takes the croup, nor break my heart when papa gets into the 'Gazette.' Have you found it? Why, it's under your hand, there. They would not cry their eyes out for me, so I can see the funny side of their adventures, bless them!"

"Is this it, ma'am?"

"There are but two books in the box. Has it an I and a V on the back?"

"V, O, L, I, V," spelled out old Mildred, who was listening in a fever for the sounds of Charles Fairfield's arrival.

"That's it. That's the book you should read. I take it in, and I hire all the others, and a French one, from the Hoxton library. I make Molly Jinks, the little, dirty, starving maid, read to me two hours a day. She's got rather to like it. How are your eyes?"

"I can make out twelve or fourteen verses wi' the glasses, but not more, at one bout."

"Well, get on your glasses. This is the 'Magazine of the Beau-Monde, and Court and Vashionable Gazette,' and full of pictures. Turn over."

"La, ma'am, 'tis beautiful, but what have
I to do with the like?"

"Well, look out for the *puce gros de
Naples* walking dress, about page twenty-
nine, and I'll show you the picture afterwards. Do be quick. I have had it four
years, it's quite good though, only I'm grown
a little fuller since, and it don't fit now. So
read it, and you'll see how I'll dress
you."

And bending her head forward and knitting her brows, she listened absorbed, while
old Mildred helped, or corrected, at every
second word, by her blind patroness, babbled
and stuttered on with her in duet recitation.

"Walking dress," said Mildred—

"Go on," said the lady, who, having this
like other descriptions in that cherished
work pretty well by heart, led off ener-
getically with her lean old companion, and
together they read—

"A *pelisse* of puce-coloured *gros de Naples*,
the corsage made to sit close to the shape,

with a large round pelerine which wraps across in front. The sleeve is excessively large at the upper part of the arm. The fulness of the lower is more moderate. It is confined in three places by bands and terminated by a broad wrist-band. The pelerine and bands of the sleeves are cased with satin to correspond, and three satin *rouleaus* are arranged *en tablier* on the front of the skirt. The bonnet is of rice straw of the cottage shape, trimmed under the brim on the right side, with a band and *nœud* of gold-coloured ribbon. The crown being also ornamented with gold-coloured ribbon, and a sprig of lilac, placed perpendicularly. Half-boots of black *gros de Naples*, tipped with black kid."

Here they drew breath, and Mildred Tarnley was silent for a minute, thinking how much more like a lady her mother used to dress than *she* was able, and what fine presents of old clothes old Mrs. Fairfield used to send her now and then from

Wyvern. For a moment an air of dignity, a sense of feminine vanity, showed itself in the face and mien of Mrs. Tarnley.

"That rice straw bonnet, with the gold-coloured *nœud*, of course I haven't got, nor the *gros de Naples'* boots—they're gone, of course, long ago; but it reads best, altogether, and I hadn't the heart to stop you, nor you to stop reading till we got to the end. And look at the pictures, you'll easily find it; and I'll write and have the pelisse sent here by the day-coach. It will be here on Sunday. Do you like it?"

"It is a bit too fine for me, I'm afraid," said Mildred, smiling in spite of herself, with a grim elation; "my poor mother used to dress herself grand enough, in her day, and keep me handsome also when I was a young thing. But since the ladies come no more to Carwell the Grange has been a dull place, and gives a body enough to do to live, and little thought o' fine dresses, and few to see them, except o' Sundays, if 'twas here; not but 'twould be more for the credit o' the family if old Mildred Tarnley, that's known down here for housekeeper at the Grange of Carwell, wasn't turned out quite so poor and dowdy, and seeing them taking the wall o' me, which their mothers used to courtesy to mine, at church and market, and come up here to the Grange as humble as you please, when money was stirring at Carwell, and I, young as I was, thought more on, a deal more, than the best o' them."

"I drink your health, Mildred; as you won't pledge me, I do it alone."

"I thank ye, ma'am." .

"Ha, yes, that does me good; I'm tired. to death, Mildred."

"There's two on us so, ma'am; shall I get you to bed, please?"

"In a minute; give me your hand again, girl; come, come, come,—yes, I have it. I think you are more friendly, eh? I *think* so; but the little goodwill I ever show you now is *nothing* to what I mean for you when I come to Wyvern—nothing."

And she strengthened the present assurance with an oath, and grasped Mildred's hard brown hand very tight.

"And you'll be kind to me, Mildred, when I want it; and I *shall* want it, mind, and I'll never forget it to you; 'twill be the making of you. I'll show you how much I trust you, for I'll put myself in your power."

And, hereupon, she shook her hand harder. Her face and manner were changed, and she looked horribly frightened for some minutes.

"I don't blame you, Mildred, but, this thing must not go on—it must not be."

Mildred in her own way looked disconcerted and even agitated at this odd speech. She screwed her mouth sharply to one side, and with her brow knit had turned a frightened gaze on her visitor.

"There's things as can't be undone, and things as can," said she, after a pause oracu-

larly; "best not meddle or make—worms
that is, and dust that will be, and God over
all."

"God over all, why not?" repeated the
old soldier vaguely, and stood up suddenly
with a kind of terrified shudder, "take me,
hold me, quick."

"A fit? La bless us," cried Tarnley,
seizing her in her lean arms.

The lady answered nothing, but grasped
her fast by the wrist and shoulder, and so
she stood for a time shuddering and swaying.
"Better at last," she said, "a little—put me
in the chair."

And she made a great shuddering sigh or
two, and called for water and "hartshorn"
and the hysteria subsided. And now she
seemed overpowered with languor, and answered faintly and in monosyllables to old
Mrs. Tarnley's uncomfortable inquiries.

"Now I shall get a sleep," she said at last,
in low drowsy tones, interrupted with heavy
sighs, and she looked so ill that old Mildred

more than ever wished her back again at
Hoxton Old Town.

"Help me to my bed—support me—get
off my things," she moaned and mumbled,
and at last lay down with a great groaning
sigh.

"What am I to do with her now?" thought
Mrs. Tarnley, who was doubtful whether in
this state she could be safely left to herself.

But the patient set her at ease upon the
point.

"Get your ear down," she whispered, "near,
near—you need not stay any longer—only—
one thing—the closet with the long row of
pegs and the three presses in it, that lies
between *her* room and mine, I remember it
well—it isn't open—I shouldn't like her to
find me here."

"No, ma'am, it ain't open, the doors were
papered over, this room and hers, as I told
you, when the rooms was done up."

The old soldier sighed and whispered—

"My head is very bad, make no noise,

dear, don't move the tray, don't touch anything—leave me to myself, and I'll sleep till
eleven o'clock to-morrow morning; but go
out softly, and then, no noise, for my sleep,"
groaned this huge woman, " is a bird's sleep
—a bird's sleep, and a pin dropping wakes
me, a mouse stirring wakes me—oh—oh—
oh. That's all." Glad to be dismissed on
these easy terms, Mildred Tarnley bid her
softly good night, having left her basket with
her sal volatile, and all other comforts, on
the table at her bedside.

And so, softly she stole on tiptoe out of
the room, and closed her door, waiting for a
moment to clear her head, and be quite sure
that the "Dutchwoman," whom they very
much hated and feared, was actually estab-
lished in her bed-room at Carwell Grange.

CHAPTER VIII.

NEWS FROM CRESSLEY COMMON.

A PRETTY medley was revolving in old Mildred's brain as she stood outside this door, on the gallery. The epileptic old soldier, the puce *gros de Naples*, Tom on outpost duty on Cressley Common—had he come back? Charles Fairfield, perhaps, in the house, and that foolish poor young wife in her room, in the centre, and herself the object of all this manœuvring and conspiring; quite unconscious. Mildred had a good many wires to her fingers just now; could she possibly work them all and keep the show going?

She was listening now, wondering whether Master Charles had arrived, wondering whether the young lady was asleep, and wondering, most of all, why she had been fool enough to meddle in other people's affairs. " What the dickens was it to her if they was all in kingdom come ? If Mildred was a roastin' they wouldn't, not one of 'em, walk across the yard there, to take her off the spit—la, bless you, not a foot."

Mildred was troubled about many things. Among others, what was the meaning of those oracular appeals of the Dutchwoman in which she had seemed to know something of the real state of things.

Down went Mildred Tarnley, softly still, for she would not risk waking Alice, and at the foot of the second staircase she paused again.

All was quiet, she peeped into Tom's little room, under the staircase. It was still empty. Into the kitchen she went, nothing had been stirred there.

From habit she trotted about, and settled and unsettled some of the scanty ironmongery and earthenware, and peeped, with her candle aloft, into this corner and that, and she removed the smoothing-iron that stood on the window-stool, holding the shutters close, and peeped into the paved yard, tufted with grass, high over which the solemn trees were drooping.

Then, candle in hand, the fidgety old woman visited the back door, the latch was in its place, and she turned about and visited the panelled sitting-room. The smell of flowers was there, and on the little spider-table was Alice's work-box, and some little muslin clippings and bits of thread and tape, the relics of that evening's solitary work over the little toilet on which her pretty fingers and sad eyes were now always employed.

Well, there was no sign of Master Charles here; so with a little more pottering and sniffing, out she went, and again to the back door, which softly she opened, and she toddled across the uneven pavement to the back-door and looked out, and walked forth upon the narrow road, that, darkened with thick trees, overhangs the edge of the ravine.

Here she listened, and listened in vain. There was nothing but the soft rush of the leaves overhead in the faint visitings of the night air, and across the glen at intervals came that ghastliest of sounds, between a long-drawn hiss and shiver, from a lonely owl.

Interrupted at intervals by this freezing sound, the old woman listened and muttered now and again a testy word or two. What was to be done, if by any mischance or blunder of Tom's the master should thunder his summons at the hall-door? Down of course would fly his young wife to let him in, and be clasped in his arms, while from the low window of the Dutchwoman that evil tenant might overhear every word that passed, and almost touch their heads with her down-stretched hand.

A pretty scene it would lead to, and agreeable consequences to Mildred herself.

"The woman's insane; she's an evil spirit; many a time she would have brained me in a start of anger if I hadn't been sharp. The mark of the cut glass decanter she flung at my head is in the doorcase at the foot of the stairs this minute like the scar of a bill-hook, the mad beast. I thank God she's blind, though there's an end o' them pranks, any-how. But she's a limb o' the evil one, and where there's a will there's a way, and blind though she be, I would not trust her."

She walked two or three steps slowly, toward Cressley Common, from which direc-tion she expected the approach of Charles Fairfield.

No wonder Mildred was fidgeted, there were so many disasters on the cards. If she could but see Charles Fairfield something at least might be guarded against. This wiry old woman was by no means hard of hearing —rather sharp, on the contrary, was her ear. But she listened long in vain.

Fearful lest something might go wrong within doors during her absence, she was turning to go back, when she thought she heard the distant clink of a horseshoe on the road.

Her old heart throbbed suddenly, and frowning as she listened, with eyes directed towards the point of approach, softly she said " hush," as if to quiet the faint rustle of the trees.

Stooping forward, she listened, with her lean arm extended, every wrinkled knuckle of her brown hand, and every black-rimmed nail distinct in the moonlight.

Yes, it was the clink of trotting horseshoes. She prayed heaven the blind woman might not hear it. There was a time when her more energetic misanthropy would possibly have enjoyed a *fracas* such as was now to be apprehended. But years teach us the value of quiet, the providential instincts of growing helplessness disarm our pugnacity, and all but quite reprobate spirits grow gentler and kinder as the hour of parting with earth approaches. Thus had old Mildred taken her part in this game, and as her stake became deeper and more dangerous her zeal burnt intensely.

Nearer and sharper came the clink, and old Mildred in her anxiety walked on, sometimes five steps, sometimes twenty, to meet the rider.

It was Tom who appeared, mounted on the mule. I think he took Mildred for a ghost, for he pulled up violently more than twenty yards away, and said, " Lord ! who's that ? "

" It's me, Tom, Mrs. Tarnley ; and is he comin' ? "

" I hardly knowed you, Mrs. Tarnley. No, I met him up near the stone."

" Not a coming ? " urged Mildred.

" No."

" Thank God. Well, and what did you tell him ? "

" I told him your message. He first asked all about the young lady, and then I told him how she was, and then I told him your message——"

" Ay ? "

"Word for word, and he drew bridle and stood a while, thinkin', and he wished to know whether the mistress had spoke with her—Mr. Harry's friend, I mean—and I said I didn't know; and he asked was the house quiet, and no high words going, nor the new comer giving any trouble, and I said *no*, so far as I knowed. Then, says he, I think, Tom, I had best let Master Harry settle it his own way, so I'll ride back again to Darwynd, and you can come over to the old place for the horse to-morrow; and tell Mildred I thank her for her care of us, and she shall hear from me in a day or two, and tell no one else, mind, that you have seen me. Well, I asked was there anything more, and he paused a bit, and says he, no, not at present. And then again, says he, tell Mildred Tarnley I'll write to her, and let her know where I am, and mind, Tom, you go yourself to the Post Office, and be sure the letters go only to the persons they are directed to, your mistress's to her, and Mildred's

to *her*, and don't you talk with that person
that I hear has come to the Grange, and if
by any chance she should get into talk with
you, you must be wide awake and tell her
nothing, and get away from her as quick as
you can.   It's easy to escape her, for she's
blind."

"So she is," affirmed Mildred, "as that
wall.   Go on."

"'Then,' says he, ' good night, Tom, get
ye home again.'   So I wished him God
speed, and I rode away, and when I was on
a bit I threw a look back again over my
shoulder, and I saw him still in the same
spot, no more stirring than the stone at the
roadside, thinking, I do suppose."

"And that's all?" said Mildred.

"That's all."

"Bring in the beast very quiet, Tom, unless
you leave him in the field for the night, and
don't be clappin' o' doors or ginglin' o' bridle
bits.   That one has an ear like a hare, and
she'll be askin' questions; and when you've

done in the stable come you in this way, and
I'll let you in softly, and don't you be talkin'
within doors above a whisper.   Your voice is
rough, and her ear is as sharp as a needle's
point."

Tom gave her a little nod and a great
wink, and got off the mule, and led him on
the grass toward the stable-yard, and old
Mildred at the same time got in softly by
the other entrance, and in the kitchen
awaited the return of Tom.

She sat by the fire, troubled in mind, with
her eyes turned askance on the windows.
What a small thing is a human body, and
what a gigantic moral sphere surrounds that
little centre!   That blind woman lay still as
death, on a sixfoot-long bedstead, in a remote
chamber.   But the direful circuit of that
sphere which radiated thence enveloped old
Mildred Tarnley go where she would, and
outspread even the bourn of the road which
Charles Fairfield was to travel that night.
For Mildred Tarnley, something of molesta-

tion and horror was in it, which forbid her
to rest.

Tom came into the yard, and Mildred was
at the door, and opened it before he could.
place his hand on the latch.

" Put off them big shoes, and not a word
above your breath, and not a stir, but get ye
in again to your bed as still as a mouse," said
Mrs. Tarnley, in a hard whisper, giving him
a shake of the shoulder.

" Ye'll gi'e me a mug o' beer, Mrs. Tarnley,
and a lump o' bread, and a cut o' cheese
wouldn't hurt me ; I'm a bit hungry. If you
won't I must even take a smoke, for I can't
sleep as I am."

" Well, I will give ye a drink and a bit o'
bread and cheese. Did ye lock the yard-
door ? "

" No," said Tom.

" Well, no, never you mind ; I'll do it," said
Mildred, stopping him, " and go you straight
to your room, and here's the lantern for you ;
and now get ye in, and not a sound, mind,

you gi'e me your pipe here, for you shan't be stinkin' the house wi' your nasty tobaccy."

So Tom was got quick to his bed.

And Mildred sat down again by the kitchen fire, to rest for a little, feeling too tired to undress.

" Well, I *do* thank God of his mercy he's *not* a comin'; I do. Who can tell what would be if he *was?*   And now, if only Master Harry was sure to keep away all might go right—yes, all—all might go right. Oh, ho, ho! I wish it was, and my old head at rest, for I'm worked worse than a horse, and wore off my feet altogether."

And all this time she was looking through the kitchen-window, with dismal eyes, from her clumsy oak chair by the fire, with her feet on the fender, and her lean shanks as close to the bars as was safe, shaking her head from time to time as she looked out on the black outlines of the trees which stood high and gloomy above the wall at the other side, against the liquid moonlit sky.

CHAPTER IX.

AN UNLOOKED-FOR RETURN.

IN spite of her troubles, as she sat by the fire, looking out through the window, fatigue overcame Mildred, and she nodded. But her brain being troubled, and her attitude uneasy, she awoke suddenly from a sinister dream, and as still unconscious where she was, her eyes opened upon the same melancholy foliage and moonlit sky and the dim enclosure of the yard, the scenery on which they had closed. She saw a pale face staring in upon her through the window. The fingers were tapping gently on the glass.

Old Mildred blinked and shook her head to get rid of what seemed to her a painful illusion.

It was Charles Fairfield who stood at

the window, looking wild and miserably
ill.

Mildred stood up, and he beckoned. She
signed toward the door, which she went
forthwith and opened.

"Come in, sir," she said.

His saddle, by the stirrup-leather, and his
bridle were in his hand. Thus he entered
the kitchen, and dropped them on the tiled
floor. She looked in his face, he looked in hers.
There was a silence. It was not Mildred's
business to open the disagreeable subject.

"Would you please like anything?"

"No, no supper, thanks. Give me a drink
of water, I'm thirsty. I'm tired, and—we're
quite to ourselves?"

"Yes, sir; but wouldn't ye better have
beer?" answered she.

"No—water—thanks."

And he drank a deep draught.

"Where's the horse, sir?" she asked after
a glance at the saddle which lay on its side
on the floor.

"In the field, the poplar field, all right—
well?"

"Tom told you my message, sir," she
asked, averting her eyes a little.

"Yes—where is she—*asleep?*"

"The mistress is in her bed, asleep I do
suppose."

"Yes, yes, and quite well, Tom says. And
where is the—the—you sent me word there
was some one here. I know whom you mean.
Where is she?"

"In the front bed-room—the old room—it
will be over the hall-door, you know—she's
in bed, and asleep, I'm thinkin'; but best
not make any stir—some folks sleep so light,
ye know."

"It's late," he said, taking out his watch,
but forgetting to consult it, "and I dare say
she *is*—she came to-night, yes—and she's
tired, or ought to be—a long way."

He walked to the window, and was looking, with the instinct which leads us always,
in dark places, to look toward the light,

above the dusky trees to the thin luminous cloud that streaked the sky.

"Pretty well tired myself, Mr. Charles; you may guess the night I've put in; I was a'most sleepin' myself when ye came to the window. Tom said ye wern't a comin'; 'tis a mercy the yard door wasn't locked; five minutes more and I'd have locked it."

"It would not have mattered much, Mildred."

"Ye'd a climbed, and pushed up the window, mayhap."

"No; I'd have walked on; a feather would have turned me from the door as it was."

He turned about and looked at her dreamily.

"On *where?*" she inquired.

"On, anywhere; on into the glen. If you are tired, Mildred, so am I."

"You need a good sleep, Master Charles."

"A long sleep, Mildred. I'm tired. I had

a mind as it was to walk on and trouble you here no more."

"Walk on—hoot! nonsense, Mr. Charles; 'tisn't come to that; giving up your house to a one like her."

"I wish I was dead, Mildred. I don't know whether it was a good or an evil angel that turned me in here. I'd have been easier by this time if I had gone on, and had my leap from the scaur to the bottom of the glen."

"None o' that nonsense, man!" said Mildred, sternly; "ye ha' brought that poor young lady into a doubtful pass, and ye must stand by her, Charles. You're come of no cowardly stock, and ye shan't gi'e her up, and your babe that's comin', poor little thing to shame and want for lack of a man's heart under your ribs. I say, I know nout o' the rights of it; but God will judge ye if ye leave her now."

High was Mrs. Tarnley's head, and very grim she looked as with her hand on his shoulder she shook up "Master Charles" from the drowse of death.

"I won't, old Tarnley," he said at last. "You're right—poor little Alice, the loving little thing!"

He turned suddenly again to the window and wept in silence strange tears of agony.

Old Tarnley looked at him sternly askance. I don't think she had much pity for him; she was in nowise given to the melting mood, and hardly knew what that sort of whimpering meant.

"I say," she broke out, "I don't know the rights of it, how should I? but this I believe, if you thought you were truly married to that woman that's come to-night, you'd never a found it in your heart to act such a villain's part by the poor, young, foolish creature up stairs, and make a sham wife o' her."

"Never, never, by heaven. I'm no more that wretched woman's husband than I'm married to you."

"Mildred knew better than marry any-

one ; there's little I see but tears and wrin-
kles, and oftentimes rags and hunger comes
of it ; but 'twill be done, marryin' and givin'
in marriage, says the Scriptures, 'tis so now,
'twas so when Noah went into the ark, and
'twill be so when the day of judgment breaks
over us."

"Yes," said Charles Fairfield, abstractedly ;
" of course that miserable woman sticks at no
assertion ; her idea is simply to bully her
way to her object. It doesn't matter what
she says, and it never surprised me. I
always knew if she lived she'd give me
trouble one day ; but that's all ; just trouble,
but no more ; not the slightest chance of
succeeding—not the smallest ; she knows it ;
I know it. The only thing that vexes me is
that people who know all about it as well as
I do, and people who, of all others, should
feel for me, and feel with me, should talk as
if they had doubts upon the subject now."

"I didn't say so, Master Charles," said
Mildred.

"I didn't mean you, I meant others, quite a different person; I'm utterly miserable; at a more unlucky moment all this could not have happened by any possibility."

"Well, I'm sure I never said it; I never thought but one thing of her; the foul-tongued wicked beast."

"Don't you talk that way of her," said Charles, savagely. "Whatever she is she has suffered, she has been cruelly used, and I am to blame for all. I did not mean it, but it is all my fault."

Mrs. Tarnley sneered, but said nothing, and a silence followed.

"I know," he said, in a changed way, "you mean kindly to me."

"Be kind to yourself. I hold it's the best way in this bleak world, Mr. Charles. I never was thanked for kindness yet."

"You have always been true to me, Mildred, in your own way—in your own way, mind, but always true, and I'll show you yet, if I'm spared, that I can be grateful. You know how I am now—no power to serve anyone—no power to show my regard."

" I don't complain o' nothing," said Mildred.

" Has my brother been here, Mildred ? " he asked.

" Not he."

" No letters for me ? " asked he.

" Nothing, sir."

" You never get a lift when you want it— never," said Charles, with a bitter groan ; "never was a fellow driven harder to the wall—never a fellow nearer his wits' ends. I'm very glad, Mildred, I have some one to talk to—one old friend. I don't know what to do—I can't make up my mind to anything, and if I hadn't you just now, I think I should go distracted. I have a great deal to ask you. That lady, you say, has been in her room some time—did she talk loud—was she angry—was there any noise ? "

" No, sir."

" Who saw her ? "

"No one but myself, and the man as drove her."

"Thank God for that. Does she know about my—did she hear that your mistress is in the house ?"

"I said she was Master Harry's wife, and told her, Lord forgive me, that he was here continually, and you hardly ever, and then only for a few hours at a time."

"That's very good—she believed it ?"

"Every word, so far as I could see. I a' told a deal o' lies."

"Well, well, and what more ?"

"And the beginning of sin is like the coming in of waters, and 'twill soon make an o'er wide gap for itself, and lay all under."

"Yes—and—and—you really think she believed all you said ?"

"Ay, I do," answered she.

"Thank God, again ! " said he, with a deep sigh. "Oh, Mildred, I wish I could think what's best to be done. There are ever so many things in my head."

She felt a trembling she thought in the hand he laid upon her arm.

"Take a drink o' beer, you're tired, sir," said she.

"No, no—not much—never mind, I'm better as I am. How has your mistress been?"

"Well, midlin'—pretty well."

"I wish she was quite well, Mildred—it's very unlucky. If the poor little thing were only quite well, it would make everything easy; but I daren't frighten her—I daren't tell her—it might be her death. Oh, Mildred, isn't all this terrible?"

"Bad enough—I can't deny."

"Would it be better to run that risk and tell her everything?" he said.

"Well, it *is* a risk, an' a great one, and it might be the same as puttin' a pistol to her head and killin' her; 'tis a tryin' time with her, poor child, and a dangerous bed, and mind ye this, if there's any talk like that, and the crying and laughing fits mayhap that

comes with it, don't ye think but the old cat
will hear it, and then in the wild talk a's
out in no time, and the fat in the fire; no,
if she's to hear it, it can't be helped, and the
will o' God be done; but if I was her
husband, I'd sooner die than tell her, being
as she is."

"No, of course, no—she must not be told;
I'm sure you're right, Mildred. I wish Harry
was here, he thinks of things sometimes, that
don't strike me. I wish Harry would come,
he might think of something—he would,
I dare say—he would, I'm certain."

"I wish that woman was back again where
she came from," said Mildred, from whose
mind the puce *gros de Naples* was fading,
for she had a profound distrust of her
veracity, and the pelisse looked very like a
puce-coloured lie.

"Don't Mildred—don't, like a good creature—you won't for my sake, speak harshly
of that unhappy person," he said gently this
time, and laying his hand on her shoulder.

"I'm glad you are here, Mildred—I'm very glad; I remember you as long as I can remember anything—you were always kind to me, Mildred—always the same—true as steel."

He was speaking with the friendliness of distress. It is in pain that sympathy grows precious, and with the yearning for it, returns something of the gentleness and affection of childhood.

"She's come for no good," said Mildred, " she's sly, and she's savage, and if you don't mind me saying so, I often thought she was a bit mad—folk as has them fits, ye know, they does get sometimes queerish."

"We can talk of her by-and-by," said he; " what was in my mind was about a different thing. For a thousand reasons I should hate a *fracas*—I mean a row with that person at present; you know yourself how it might affect the poor little thing up stairs. Oh, my darling, my darling, what have I brought you into?"

"Well, well, no help for spilled milk," said Mildred. "What was you a-thinking of?"

"Oh, yes, thank you, Mildred—I was thinking—yes—if your mistress was well enough for a journey, I'd take her away from this—I'd take her away immediately—I'd take her quite out of the reach of that—that restless person. I ought to have done so at once, but I was so miserably poor, and this place here to receive us, and who could have fancied she'd have dreamed, in her state of health, and with her affliction—her sight, you know—of coming down here again ; but I'm the unluckiest fellow on earth ; I never, by any chance, leave a blot that isn't hit. Don't you think, Mildred, I had better not wake your mistress to-night to talk over plans ?"

"Don't you go near her ; a sight of your face would tell her all wasn't right."

"I had better not see her, you think ?"

"*Don't* see her. So soon as you know yourself what you're going to do with her,

and if you make up your mind to-night so
much the better—write you to tell her what
she's to do, and give me the letter and I'll give
it to her as if it came by a messenger; and
take you my counsel—don't you stop here a
minute longer than you can. Leave before
daybreak, you're no use here, and if she finds
you 'twill but make bad worse. When will
ye lie down—you'll not be good for nothin'
to-morrow if ye don't sleep a bit—lie down
on the sofa in the parlour, and your cloak is
hangin' in the passage, and be you out o'
the house by daybreak, and I'll have a bit o'
breakfast ready before ye go."

"And there's Lady Wyndale, I didn't tell
you, offered to take care of Alice, your mistress, and she need only go there for the
present; but that might be too near, and I
was thinking it might not do."

"Best out o' reach altogether when ye go
about it," said Mildred. "Sit here if you
like it, or lie down, as I said, in the parlour,
and if you settle your mind on any plan just

knock at my door, and I'll have my clothes
about me and be ready at call, and Tom's in
his old crib under the stair, if you want him to
get the saddle on the horse, and I won't take
down the fire, I'll have it handy for your
breakfast, and now I can't stop talkin' no
longer, for Mildred's wore off her feet—will
ye take a candle, or will ye stop here ? "

"Yes, give me a candle, Mildred—thanks
—and don't mind the cloak, I'll get it myself,
I will lie down a little, and try to sleep—I
wish I could—and if you waken shake me up
in an hour or two, something must be settled
before I leave this, something *shall* be settled,
and that poor little creature out of reach of
trouble and insult. Don't forget. Good
night, Mildred, and God bless you, Mildred,
God for ever bless you."

CHAPTER X.

CHARLES FAIRFIELD talked of sleeping. There was little chance of that. He placed the candle on one of the two old oak cupboards, as they were still called, which occupied corresponding niches in the wainscoted wall, opposite the fireplace, and he threw himself at his length on the sofa.

Tired enough for sleep he was; but who can stop the mill of anxious thought into which imagination pours continually its proper grist? In his tired head its wheels went turning, and its hammers beat with monotonous pulsation and whirl—weariest and most wasting of fevers!

He turned his face, like the men of old, in

his anguish, to the wall. Then he tried the
other side, wide awake, and literally staring,
from point to point, in the fear and fatigue of
his vain ruminations. Then up he sat, and
flung his cloak on the floor, and then to the
window he went, and, opening the shutter,
looked out on the moonlight, and the peaceful
trees that seemed bowed in slumber, and
stood, hardly seeing it—hardly thinking in
his confused misery.

One hand in his pocket, the other against
the window-case, to which the stalworth good
fellow, Harry, had leaned his shoulder in their
unpleasant dialogue and altercation. Harry,
his chief stay, his confidant and brother—
dare he trust him now? If he might, where
could he find him? Better do his own work
—better do it indifferently than run a risk of
treason. He did not quite know what to
make of Harry.

So with desultory resolution he said to
himself, "Now I'll think in earnest, for I've
got but two hours to decide in." There was

a pretty little German village, quite out of
the ordinary route of tourists. He remembered its rocks and hills, its ruined castle and
forest scenery, as if he had seen them but
yesterday—the very place for Alice, with her
simple tastes and real enjoyment of nature.
On that point, though under present circumstances by short journeys, they should effect
their retreat.

In three hours' time he would himself
leave the Grange. In the meantime he must
define his plans exactly. He must write
to Harry—he must write to Alice, for he
was quite clear he would not see her;
and, after all, he might have been making a
great deal too much of this odious affair,
which, rightly managed, might easily end in
smoke.

Pen, ink, and paper he found, and now to
clear his head and fix his attention. Luckily
he had a hundred pounds in his pocket-book.
Too hard that out of his miserable pittance,
scarcely five hundred pounds a year, he

should have to pay two hundred pounds to that woman, who never gave him an easy week, and who seemed bent on ruining him if she could. By the dull light of the mutton-fat with which Mildred had furnished him he wrote this note—

"MY DARLING LITTLE WOMAN,—

"You must make Dulcibella pack up your things. Tom will have a chaise here at eleven o'clock. Drive to Wykeford and change horses there, and go on to Lonsdale, where I will meet you *at last*. Then and there your own, poor, loving Ry will tell you all his plans and reasons for this sudden move. We must get away by easy stages, and baffle possible pursuit, and then a quiet and comparatively happy interval for my poor little fluttered bird. I live upon the hope of our meeting. Out of reach of all trouble we shall soon be, and your poor Ry happy, where only he can be happy, in your dear presence. I enclose ten pounds. Pay *nothing and nobody* at the Grange. Say I told you so. You will reach Lonsdale, if you leave Carwell not later than eleven, before five. Don't delay to pack up any more than you actually want. Leave all in charge of old Mildred, and we can easily write in a day or two for anything we may want.

"Ever, my own idolized little woman,

"Your own poor adoring

"Ry."

So this was finished, and now for Harry:

"My dear Harry,—

"How you must hate the sight of my hand. I never write but to trouble you. But, as you will perceive, I am myself in trouble more than enough to warrant my asking you again to aid me if it should lie in your way. You will best judge if you can, and how you can. The fact is that what you apprehended turns out to be too true. That person who, however I may have been at one time to blame, has certainly no right to charge me with want of generosity or consideration, seems to have made up her mind to give me all the annoyance in her power. She is at this moment *here* at Carwell Grange. I was absent when she arrived, and received timely notice, and perhaps ought to have turned about, but I could not do that without ascertaining first exactly how matters stood at Carwell. So I am here, without any one's being aware of it except old Mildred, who tells me that the person in question is under the impression that it is *you*—and not *I* —who are married, and that it is your wife who is residing in the house. As you have been no party to this deception, pray let her continue to think so. I shall leave this before daybreak, my visit not having exceeded four hours. I leave a note for poor little Alice, telling her to follow me to-morrow—I should say *this* morning—to

Lonsdale, where I shall meet her ; and thence
we get on to London, and from London, my
present idea is, to make our way to some
quiet little place on the Continent, where I
mean to stay quite concealed until circumstances alter for the better. What I want
you, and *beg* of you to do for me at present,
is just this—to sell *everything* at Carwell that
is saleable—the horse, the mule, the two
donkeys, the carts, plough, &c., &c., in fact
everything out of doors ; and let the farm to
Mildred's nephew, who wanted to take it last
year. It is, including the garden, nineteen
acres. I wish him to have it, provided he
pays a fair rent, because I think he would be
kind to his aunt, old Mildred. He must sti-
pulate to give her her usual allowances of
vegetables, milk, and all the rest from the
farm ; and she shall have her room, and the
kitchen, and her 8*l*. a year as usual. Do
like a good old fellow see to this, and try to
turn all you can into money for me. I shall
have miserably little to begin with, and any-

thing you can get together will be a lift to me. If you write under cover to J. Dylke at the old place in Westminster, it will be sure to reach me. I don't know whether all this is intelligible. You may guess how distracted I am and miserable. But there is no use in describing. I ought to beg your pardon a thousand times for asking you to take all the trouble involved in this request. But, dear Harry, you will ask yourself who else on earth has the poor devil to look to in an emergency but his brother? I know my good Harry will remember how urgent the case is. Any advice you can spare me in my solitary trouble will be most welcome. I think I have said everything—at least all I can think of in this miserable hurry—I feel so helpless. But you are a clever fellow, and always were—so much cleverer than I, and know how to manage things. God bless you, dear Harry, I know you won't forget how pressed I am. You were always prompt in my behalf, and I never so needed a friend like you—for delay here might lead to the worst annoyances.

"Ever, dear Harry, your affectionate brother,

"CHARLES FAIRFIELD.

"Carwell Grange."

It was a relief to his mind when these letters were off it, and something like the rude outline of a plan formed.

Very tired was Charles Fairfield when he had folded and addressed his letters. No physical exertion exhausts like the monotonous pain of anxiety. For many nights he had had no sleep, but those wearying snatches of half-consciousness in which the same troublous current is still running through the brain, and the wasted nerves of endurance are still tasked. He sat now in his chair, the dim red light of the candle at his elbow, the window shutter open before him, and the cold serene light of the moon over the outer earth and sky.

Gazing on this, a weary sleep stole over his senses, and for a full hour the worn-out man slept profoundly.

Into this slumber slowly wound a dream, of which he could afterwards remember only that it was somehow horrible.

Dark and direful grew his slumber thus visited; and in a way that accorded well with its terrors, he was awakened.

CHAPTER XI.

AWAKE.

In his dream, a pale frightened face approached him slowly, and recoiling uttered a cry. The scream was horribly prolonged as the figure receded. He thought he recognised some one—dead or living he could not say—in the strange, Grecian face, fixed as marble, that with enormous eyes, had looked into his.

With this sound ringing in his ears he awoke. As is the case with other over-fatigued men, on whom, at length, slumber has seized, he was for a time in the attitude of wakefulness before his senses and his recollection were thoroughly aroused, and his dream quite dissipated. Another long shriek, and another, and another, he heard.

Charles recognised, he fancied, his wife's voice. Scared, and wide awake, he ran from the room—to the foot of the stairs— up the stairs. A tread of feet he heard in the room, and the door violently shaken, and another long, agonized scream.

Over this roof and around it is the serenest and happiest night. The brilliant moon, the dark azure and wide field of stars make it a night for holy thoughts, and lovers' vigils, so tender and beautiful. There is no moaning night-wind, not even a rustle in the thick ivy. The window gives no sound, except when the gray moth floating in its shadow taps softly on the pane. You can hear the leaf that drops of itself from the tree-top, and flits its way from bough to spray to the ground.

Even in that gentle night there move, however, symbols of guilt and danger. While the small birds, with head under wing, nestle in their leafy nooks, the white owl glides with noiseless wing, a murderous phantom,

L 2

cutting the air. The demure cat creeps on and on softly as a gray shadow till its green eyes glare close on its prey. Nature, with her gentleness and cruelty, her sublimity and meanness, resembles that microcosm, the human heart, in which lodge so many contrarieties, and the shabby contends with the heroic, the diabolic with the angelic.

In this still night Alice's heart was heavy. Who can account for those sudden, silent, but terrible changes in the spiritual vision which interpose as it were a thin coloured medium between ourselves and the realities that surround us—how all objects, retaining their outlines, lose their rosy glow and golden lights, and on a sudden fade into dismallest gray and green?

"Dulcibella, do you think he's coming? Oh! Dulcibella, do you think he'll come to-night?"

"He may, dear. Why shouldn't he? Lie down, my child, and don't be sitting up in your bed so. You'll never go asleep while you're listening and watching. Nothing but fidgets, and only the wider awake the longer you watch. *Well* I know it, and many a long hour I laid awake myself expectin' and listenin' for poor Crane a comin' home with the cart from market, long ago. He had his failin's—as who has not? poor Crane—but an honest man, and good-natured, and would not hurt a fly, and never a wry word out of his mouth, exceptin', maybe, one or two, which he never meant them, when he was in liquor, as who is there, Miss Ally, will not be sometimes? But he was a kind, handsome fellow, and sore was my heart when he was taken," and Dulcibella wiped her eyes. "Seven-and-twenty years agone last Stephen's Day I buried him in Wyvern Churchyard, and I tried to keep the little business agoin', but I couldn't make it pay no how, and when it pleased God to take my little girl six years after, I gave all up and went to live at the vicarage. But as I was sayin', miss, many a long hour I sat up a watchin' for my poor

Crane on his way home. He would sometimes stop a bit on the way, wi' a friend or
two, at the Cat and Fiddle—'twas the only
thing I could ever say wasn't quite as I could
a' liked in my poor Crane. And that's how
I came to serve your good mother, miss, and
your poor father, the good vicar o' Wyvern—
there's not been none like him since, not one
—no, indeed."

"You remember mamma very well ? "

"Like yesterday, miss," said old Dulcibella,
who often answered that question. "Like
yesterday, the pretty lady. She always looked
so pleasant, too—a smiling face, like the light
of the sun coming into a room."

"I wonder, Dulcibella, there was no picture."

"No picture. No miss. Well, ye see,
Miss Ally, dear, them pictures, I'm told,
costs a deal o' money, and they were only
beginnin' you know, and many a little ex-
pense — and Wyvern Vicarage is a small
livelihood at best, and ye must be managin'

if ye'd keep it—and good to the poor they was with all that, and gave what many a richer one wouldn't, and never spared trouble for them; they counted nothin' trouble for no one. They loved all, and lived to one another, not a wry word ever; what one liked t'other loved, and all in the light o' God's blessin'. I never seen such a couple, never; they doated on one another, and loved all, and they two was like one angel."

"Lady Wyndale has a picture of poor mamma—very small—what they call a miniature. I think it quite beautiful. It was taken when she was not more than seventeen. Lady Wyndale, you know, was ever so much elder than mamma."

"Ay, so she was, ten year and more, I dare say," answered Dulcibella.

"She is very fond of it—too fond to give it to me now; but she says, kind aunt, she has left it to me in her will. And oh! Dulcibella, I feel so lonely."

"Lonely! why should you, darling, wi' a

fine handsome gentleman to your husband, that will be squire o' Wyvern—think o' that —squire o' Wyvern, and that's a greater man than many a lord in Parliament; and he's good-natured, never a hard word or a skew look, always the same quiet way wi' him. Hoot, miss! ye mustn't be talkin' that way. Think o' the little baby that's a comin'. Ye won't know yourself for joy when ye see his face, please God, and I'm a longin' to show him to ye."

"You good old Dulcibella," said the young lady, and her eyes filled with tears as she smiled. "But poor mamma died when I was born, and oh, Dulcibella, do you think I shall ever see the face of the poor little thing? Oh! wouldn't it be sad! wouldn't it be sad!"

"Ye're not to be talkin' that nonsense, darling; 'tis sinful, wi' all that God has given you, a comfortable house over your head, and enough to eat, and good friends, and a fine, handsome husband that's kind to you, and a

blessed little child a comin' to make every
minute pleasant to all that's in the house.
Why, 'tis a sin to be frettin' like that, and as
for this thing or that thing, or being afeard,
why, everyone's afeard, if they'd let themselves, and not one in a thousand comes by
any harm ; and 'tis sinful, I tell ye, for ye
know well ye're in the hands o' the good
God that's took care o' ye till now, and took
ye out o' the little. nursery o' Wyvern Vicarage, when ye weren't the length o' my arm,
and not a friend near but poor, foolish, old
Dulcibella, that did not know where to turn.
And your aunt, that only went out as poor
as your darling mamma, brought home well
again from t'other end of the world, and well
to do, your own loving kith and kin, and good
friends raised up on every side, and the old
squire, Harry o' Wyvern, although he be a
bit angered for a while he's another good
friend, that will be sure to make it up, whatever it is came between him and Master
Charles. Hot blood's not the worst blood ;

better a blow in haste and a shake hands
after than a smile at the lips and no goodwill
wi' it. I tell you, they're not the worst, they
hot-headed, hard-fisted, out-spoken folk ; and
I'll never forget that day to him, when he
brought you home that had no home, and me
that was thinkin' o' nout but the workhouse.
So do or say what he will, God bless him for
that day, say I, for 'twas an angel's part he
did," said old Dulcibella.

"So I feel, God knows; so I feel," said
Alice, " and I hope it may all be made up ;
I'm sure it will; and, oh! Dulcibella, I have
been the cause of so much sorrow and bitter-
ness!"

She stopped suddenly, her eyes full of
tears ; but she restrained them.

"That's the way ye'll always be talking.
I'd like to know where they'd be without you.
Every man that marries will have care, more
or less; 'tis the will o' God ; and if he hadn't
he'd never think o' Him ; and 'tis a short life
at the longest, and a sore pilgrimage at the

best. So what He pleases to lay on us we must even bear wi' a patient heart, if we can't wi' a cheerful; for wi' his blessin' 'twill all end well."

"Amen," said Alice, with a cheerier smile but a load still at her heart; "I hope so, my good old Dulcibella. What should I do without you? *Wait!* hush! Is that a noise outside? No; I thought I heard a horse's tread, but there's nothing. It's too late now; there's no chance of him to-night. Do you think, Dulcibella, there is any chance?"

"Well, no, my dear; it's gettin' on too late—a deal too late; no, no, we must even put that clean out of our heads. Ye'll not get a wink o' sleep if you be listening for him. Well I know them fidgets, and many a time I lay on my hot ear—now this side, now that, listening, till I could count the veins o' my head beating like a watch, and myself only wider and wider awake every hour, and more fool I; and well and hearty home wi' him, time enough, and not a minute sooner for all my watching. And mind ye, what I often told ye when ye were a wee thing, and ye'll find it true to the end o' your days—a watch-pot never boils."

Alice laughed gently.

"I believe you are right, Dulcibella. No, he won't come to night. It was only a chance, and I might have known. But, perhaps, to-morrow? Don't you think to-morrow?"

"Very like, like enough, to-morrow—daylight, mayhap to breakfast—why not?" she answered.

"Well, I do think he may; he said, perhaps to-night, and I know, I'm sure he'll think how his poor wife is watching and longing to see him; and, as you advise, I'll put that quite out of my head; he has so many things to look after, and he only said *perhaps*; and you think in the morning. Well, I won't let myself think so, it would be too delightful; I won't think it. But it can't be many days, I'm sure—and—I won't keep you up any longer, dear old Dulcibella. I've been very selfish. So, good-night."

And they kissed, as from little Allie's infancy they had always done, before settling for the night.

" Good-night, and God love it ; it mustn't be frettin', and God bless you, my darling Miss Allie ; and you must get to sleep, or you'll be looking so pale and poor in the morning, he won't know you when he comes."

So, with another hug and a kiss they parted, and old Dulcibella leaving her young mistress's candle burning on the table, as was her wont, being nervous when she was alone, and screened from her eyes by the curtain, with a final good-night and another blessing she closed the door.

Is there ever an unreserved and complete confidence after marriage ? Even to kind old Dulcibella she could not tell all. As she smiled a little farewell on the faithful old soul her heart was ready to burst. She was longing for a good cry all to herself, and now, poor little thing, she had it.

She cried herself, as children do, to sleep.

An hour later the old grange was silent as the neighbouring churchyard of Carwell. But there was not a household in the parish, or in the county, I suppose, many of whose tenants, at that late hour, were so oddly placed.

In his chair in the oak-panelled room, down stairs, sat Charles Fairfield, in that slumber of a tormented and exhausted brain, which in its first profound submersion, resembles the torpor of apoplexy.

In his forsaken room lay on the pillow the pale face of his young wife, her eyelashes not yet dry, fallen asleep in the sad illusion of his absence—better, perhaps, than his presence would have been, if she had known but all.

In her crib down stairs, at last asleep, lay the frightened Lilly Dogger, her head still under the coverlet, under which she had popped it in panic, as she thought on the possible return of the tall unknown, and the lobe of her ear still flaming from the discipline of her vice-like pinch.

Under his slanting roof, in the recess of the staircase, with only his coat off, stretched on the broad of his back, with one great horny hand half shut under his bullet head, and the other by his side, snored honest Tom, nothing the less soundly for his big mug of beer and his excursion to Cressly Common.

For a moment now we visit the bedside of good old Dulcibella. An easy conscience, a good digestion, and an easy place in this troublesome world, are favourable to sound slumbers, and very tranquilly she slept, with a large handkerchief pinned closely about her innocent bald head, and a night-cap of many borders outside it. Her thick, well-thumbed Bible, in which she read some half-dozen verses every night, lay, with her spectacles upon its cover, on the table by the brass candlestick.

Mildred Tarnley, a thin figure with many corners, lay her length in her clothes, her old brown stuff gown her cap and broad faded ribbons binding her busy head, and her darned black worsted stockings still on her weary feet, ready at call to jump up, pop her feet again into her misshapen shoes, and resume her duties.

In her own solitary chamber, at the deserted side of the house, the tall stranger, arrayed in a white woollen night-dress, lay her length, not stirring.

After Mildred Tarnley had got herself stiffly under her quilt, she was visited with certain qualms about this person, recollections of her abhorred activity and energy in old times, and fears that the "grim white woman" was not resting in her bed. This apprehension grew so intense that, tired as she was, she could not sleep. The suspicion that, barefooted, listening, that dreadful woman was possibly groping her way through the house made her heart beat faster and faster.

At last she could bear it no longer, and up she got, lighted her candle with a match, and in her stockings glided softly through the passage, and by the room where Charles Fairfield was at that time at his letters.

He recognised the step to which his ear was accustomed, and did not trouble himself to inquire what she was about.

So, softly, softly, softly—Mildred Tarnley found herself at the door of the unwelcome guest and listened. You would not have supposed old Mildred capable of a nervous tremble, but she was profoundly afraid of this awful woman, before whose superior malignity and unearthly energy her own temper and activity quailed. She listened, but could hear no evidence of her presence. Was the woman there at all ? Lightly, lightly, with her nail, she tapped at the door. No answer. Then very softly she tried the door. It was secured.

But was the old soldier in the room still, or wandering about the house with who could fathom what evil purpose in her head ?.

The figure in white woollen was there still; she had been lying on her side, with her pale features turned toward the door as Mildred approached. Her blind eyes were moving in their sockets—there was a listening smile on her lips—and she had turned her neck awry to get her ear in the direction of the door. She was just as wide awake as Mildred herself.

Mildred watched for a time at the door, irresolute. Excuse enough, she bethought her, in the feeble state in which she had left her, had she for making her a visit. Why should she not open the door boldly and enter ? But Mildred, in something worse than solitude, was growing more and more nervous. What if that tall, insane miscreant were waiting at the door, in a fit of revenge for her suspected perfidy, ready to clutch her by the throat as she opened it, and to strangle her on the bed ? And when there came from the interior of the room a weary bleating "heigh-ho!" she absolutely bounced backward, and for a moment froze with terror.

She took a precaution as she softly withdrew. The passage, which is terminated by the "old soldier's" room, passes a dressing-room on the left, and then opens, on the other side, upon a lobby. This door is furnished with a key, and having secured it, Mrs. Tarnley, with that key in her pocket, felt that she had pretty well imprisoned that evil spirit, and returned to her own bed more serenely, and was soon lost in slumber.

CHAPTER XII.

RESTLESS.

SOME lean, nervous temperaments, once fairly excited, and in presence of a substantial cause of uneasiness, are very hard to reduce to composure. After she had got back again, Mildred Tarnley fidgeted and turned in her bed, and lay in the dark, with her tired eyes wide open, and imagining, one after another, all sorts of horrors.

She was still in her clothes; so she got up again, and lighted a candle, and stole away, angry with herself and all the world on account of her fussy and feverish condition, and crept up the great stairs, and stealthily reached again the door of the "old soldier's" room.

Not a sound, not a breath, could she hear

from within. Gently she opened the door which no longer resisted. The fire was low in the grate ; and, half afraid to look at the bed, she raised the candle and did look.

There lay the "Dutchwoman," so still that Mrs. Tarnley felt a sickening doubt as she stared at her.

"Lord bless us ! she's never quite well. I wish she was somewhere else," said Mrs. Tarnley, frowning sharply at her from the door.

Then, with a little effort of resolution, she walked to the bedside, and fancied, doubt-fully, that she saw a faint motion as of breathing in the great resting figure, and she placed her fingers upon her arm, and then passed them down to her big hand, which to her relief was warm.

At the touch the woman moaned and turned a little.

"Faugh ! what makes her sleep so like dead ? She'd a frightened me a'most, if I did not know better. Some folks can't do nout like no one else." And Mildred would have liked to shake her up and bid her "snore like other people, and give over her unnatural ways."

But she did look so pale and fixed, and altogether so unnatural, that Mrs. Tarnley's wrath was overawed, and, rather uneasily, she retired, and sat for a while at the kitchen fire, ruminating and grumbling.

"If she's a-goin' to die, what for should she come all the way to Carwell? Wasn't Lonnon good enough to die in?"

Mrs. Tarnley only meant to warm her feet on the fender for a few minutes. But she fell asleep, and wakened, it might be, a quarter of an hour later, and got up and listened.

What was it that overcame old Mildred on this night with so unusual a sense of danger and panic at the presence of this woman? She could not exactly define the cause. But she was miserably afraid of her, and full of unexplainable surmises.

"I can't go to bed till I try again; I can't. I don't know what's come over me. It seems to me, Lor' be wi' us! as if the Evil One was in the house, and I don't know what I should do—and there's nout o' any avail I can do; but quiet I can't bide, and sleep won't stay wi' me while she's here, and I'll just go up again to her room, and if all's right then, I will lie down, and take it easy for the rest o' the night, come what, come may; for my old bones is fairly wore out, and I can't hold my head up no longer."

Thus resolved, and sorely troubled, the old woman took the candle again and sallied forth once more upon her grizzly expedition.

From the panelled sitting-room, where by this time Charles Fairfield sat in his chair locked in dismal sleep, came the faint red mist of his candle's light, and here she paused to listen for a moment. Well, all was quiet there, and so on and into the passage, and so into the great hall, as it

was called, which seemed to her to have
grown chill and cheerless since she was last
there, and so again cautiously up the great
stair, with its clumsy banister of oak, relieved at every turn by a square oak block
terminating in a ball, like the head of a
gigantic nine-pin.　Black looked the passage
through this archway, at the summit of this
ascent ; and for the first time Mildred was
stayed by the sinking of a superstitious
horror.

It was by putting a kind of force upon
herself that she entered this dark and silent
gallery, so far away from every living being
in the house, except that one of whom secretly she stood in awe, as of something not
altogether of this earth.

This gallery is pretty large, and about
midway is placed another arch, with a door-
case, and a door that is held open by a hook,
and, as often happens in old houses, a de-
scent of a couple of steps here brings you to
a different level of the floor.

There may have been a reason of some other sort for the uncomfortable introduction of so many gratuitous steps in doorways and passages, but certainly it must have exercised the wits of the comparatively slow persons who flourished at the period of this sort of architecture, and prevented the drowsiest from falling asleep on the way to their bed-rooms.

It happened that as she reached this doorway her eye was caught by a cobweb hanging from the ceiling. For a sharp old servant like Mrs. Tarnley, such festoonery has an attraction of antipathy that is irresistible; she tried to knock it with her hand, but it did not reach high enough, so she applied her fingers to loosen her apron, and sweep it down with a swoop of that weapon.

She was still looking up at the dusty cord that waved in the air, and as she did so she received a long pull by the dress, from an unseen hand below—a determined tweak—

tightening and relaxing as she drew a step back, and held the candle backward to enable her to see.

It was not her kitten, which might have playfully followed her up stairs—it was not a prowling rat making a hungry attack. A low titter accompanied this pluck at her dress, and she saw the wide pale face of the Dutchwoman turned up towards her with an odious smile. She was seated on the step, with her shoulder leaning upon the frame of the door.

" You thought I was asleep under the co-verlet," she drawled : " or awake, perhaps, in the other world—dead. I never sleep long, and I don't die easily—*see!*"

" And what for are ye out o' your bed at all, ma'am ? Ye'll break your neck in this house, if ye go walking about, wi' its cranky steps and stairs, and you blind."

" When you go blind, old Mildred, you'll find your memory sharper than you think, and steps, and corners, and doors, and chimney-pieces will come to mind like a picture. What was I about?"

"Well, what *was* ye about? Sure I am I don't know, ma'am."

"No, I'm sure you don't," said she.

"But you should be in your bed—that I know, ma'am."

Still holding her dress, and with a lazy laugh, the lady made answer—

"So should you, old lass—a pair of us gadders; but I had a reason—I wanted you, old Mildred."

"Well, ma'am, I don't know how you'd 'a found me, for I sleep in the five-cornered room, two doors away from the spicery—you'd never 'a found me."

"I'd have tried—hit or miss—I would not have stayed where I was," answered the "old soldier."

"What, not in the state room, ma'am—the finest room in the house, so 'twas always supposed!"

"So be it; I don't like it," she answered.

"Ye didn't hear no noises in't, sure?" demanded Mildred.

"Not I," said the Dutchwoman. "Another reason quite, girl."

"And what the de'il is it? It must be summat grand, I take it, that makes ye better here, sittin' on a hard stair, than lying your length on a good bed."

"Right well said, clever Mildred. What is the state-room without a quiet mind?" replied the old soldier, with an oracular smile.

"What's the matter wi' your mind, ma'am?" said Mildred testily.

"I'm not safe there from intrusion," answered the lady, with little pauses between her words to lend an emphasis to them.

"I don't know what you're afeard on, ma'am," repeated Mrs. Tarnley, whose acquaintance with fine words was limited, and who was too proud to risk a mistake.

"Well, it's just this—I won't be pried upon by that young lady."

"What young lady, ma'am?" asked Mrs.

Tarnley, who fancied she might ironically mean Miss Lilly Dogger.

"Harry Fairfield's wife, of course, what other? I choose to be private here," said the Dutch dame imperiously.

"She'll not pry—she don't pry on no one, and if she wished it, she couldn't."

"Why, there's nothing between us, woman, but the long closet where you used to keep the linen, and the broken furniture and rattle-traps" (raddle-drabs she pronounced the word), "and she'll come and peep—every woman peeps and pries" (beebs and bries she called the words)—"*I* peep and pry. She'll just pretend she never knew any one was there, and she'll walk in through the closet door, and start, and beg my pardon, and say how sorry she is, and then go off, and tell you next morning how many buttons are on my pelisse, and how many pins in my pin-cushion, and let all the world know everything about me."

"But she can't come in."

" Why ? "

" Why ?　Because, ma'am, the door is papered over."

" Fine　protection—paper ! " sneered the lady.

" I saw her door locked myself before 'twas papered over," said Mildred.

" Did you, though ? " said the lady.

" With my own eyes," insisted Mildred.

" I'd rather see it with mine," joked the blind lady.　"Well, see, we'll make a long story short.　If I consent to stay in that room, I'll lock the door that opens into it.　I'll have a room, and not a passage, if you please.　I won't be peeped on, or listened to.　If I can't choose my company I'll be alone, please."

" And what do you want, ma'am ? " asked Mildred, whose troubles were multiplying.

" Another room," said the lady, doggedly.

Mildred paused.

" Well, did I ever ! " pondered Mrs. Tarnley, reading the lady's features sharply as she spoke ; but they were sullen, and, for aught she could make out, meaningless. "Well, it will do if ye can have the key, I take it, and lock your door yourself?"

"Not so well as another room, if you'll give me one, but better than nothing."

"Come along then, ma'am, for another room's not to be had at no price, and I'll gi' ye the key."

"And then, when you lock it fast, I may sleep easy. What's that your parson used to say—'the wicked cease from troubling, and the weary are at rest.' Plenty of wicked people going, Mrs. Tarnley, and weary enough am I," sighed the great pale Dutchwoman.

"There's two on us so, ma'am," said Mildred, as she led the lady back to her room, and having placed her in her arm-chair by the fire, Mildred Tarnley took the key from a brass-headed tack, on which it hung behind the bedpost.

"Here it is, ma'am," she said, placing the key in her groping fingers.

"What key is it?" asked the old soldier.

"The key of the long linen closet that was."

"And how do I know that?" she inquired, twirling it round in her large fingers, and smiling in such a way as to nettle Mrs. Tarnley, who began—

"Ye may know, I take it, because Mildred Tarnley says so, and I never yet played a trick. I never tells lies," she concluded, pulling up on a sudden.

"Well, I know that. I know you're truth itself, so far as human nature goes; but that has its limits, and can't fly very high off the ground. Come, get me up—we'll try the key. I'll lock it myself—I'll lock it with my own fingers. Seeing is believing, and I can't see; but feeling has no fellow, and, not doubting you, Mrs. Tarnley, I'll feel for myself."

She placed her hand on Mrs. Tarnley's shoulder, and when she had reached the corner at the further side of the bed, where the covered door, as she knew, was situated, with her scissors' point, where the crevice of the door was covered over with the paper, she ripped it asunder (notwithstanding the remonstrances of Mildred, who told her she was "leavin' it not worth a rag off the road") all round the door, which thus freed, and discovering by her finger tips the point at which the keyhole was placed, she broke the paper through, introduced the key, turned it, and with very little resistance pulled the· door partly open, with an ugly grimace and a chuckle at Mildred. Then, locking it fast, she said,—

"And now I defy madam, do all she can—and you'll clap the table against it, to make more sure; and so I think I may sleep—don't you?"

Mildred scratched above her eyebrow with one finger for a moment, and she said—

"Yes, ye might a' slept, I'm thinkin', as sound before if ye had a mind, ma'am."

"What the dickens does the lass mean?"

said the blind woman, with a sleepy laugh. "As if people could sleep when they like. Why, woman, if that was so there would be no such thing as fidgets."

"Well, I suppose, no more there wouldn't—no more there wouldn't. I may take away the tray, ma'am?"

"Let it be till morning—I want rest. Good night. Are you going?—good night."

"Good night, ma'am," said Mildred, making her stiff little curtsey, although it was lost upon the lady, and a little thoughtfully she left the room.

The "Old Soldier" listened, sitting up, for she had lain down on her bed, and as she heard the click-clack of Mildred's shoe grow fainter—

"Yes, good-night really, Mildred; I think you need visit no more to-night."

And she got up, and secured the door that opened on the gallery.

"Good-night, old Tarnley," she said, with a nod and an unpleasant smirk, and then a deep and dismal sigh. Then she threw herself again upon her bed and lay still.

Old Mildred seemed also to have come to a like conclusion as to the matter of further visiting for the night, for at the door, on the step of which the Dutchwoman sitting a few minutes before had startled her, she looked back suspiciously over her shoulder, and then shutting the door noiselessly, she locked it—leaving that restless spirit a prisoner till morning.

CHAPTER XIII.

THROUGH THE WALL.

ALICE had slept quietly for some time. The old clock at the foot of the stairs had purred and struck twice since she had ceased listening and thinking. It was for all that time an unbroken sleep, and then she wakened. She had been half conscious for some time of a noise in the room, a fidgeting little noise, that teased her sleep for a time, and finally awoke her completely. She sat up in her bed, and heard, she thought, a sigh in the room. Exactly from what point she could not be certain, nor whether it was near or far.

She drew back the curtain and looked. The familiar furniture only met her view. In like manner all round the room. Encouraged by which evidence she took heart of grace, and got up, and quite to satisfy herself, made a search—as timid people will, because already morally certain that there is no need of a search.

Happily she was spared the terror of any discovery to account for the sound that had excited her uneasiness.

She turned again the key in her door, and thus secured, listened there. Everything was perfectly still. Then into bed she got, and listened to silence, and in low tones talking to herself, for the sound of her own voice was reassuring, she reasoned with her tremors, she trimmed her light and made some little clatter on the table, and bethought her that this sigh that had so much affrighted her might be no more than the slipping of one fold of her bed-curtain over another—an occurrence which she remembered to have startled her once before.

So after a time she persuaded herself that her alarm was fanciful, and she composed

herself again to sleep. Soon, however, her
evil genius began to worry her in another
shape, and something like the gnawing and
nibbling of a mouse grated on her half-
sleeping ear from the woodwork of the room.
So he sat up again, and said—

"Hish!"

Now toward the window, now toward the
fire-place, now toward the door, and all again
was quite still.

Alice got up, and throwing her dressing-
gown about her shoulders, opened the
window-shutter and looked out upon the
serene and melancholy landscape, which this
old-fashioned window with its clumsy sashes
and small panes commanded. Sweet and
sad these moonlit views that so well accord
with certain moods. But the cares at Alice's
heart were real, and returned as she quite
awoke with a renewed pang—and the cold
and mournful glory of the sky and silvered
woodlands neither cheered nor soothed her.
With a deep sigh she closed the shutter

again, and by the dusky candle-light returned to her bed. There at last she did
fall into a quiet sleep.

From this she awoke suddenly and quite.
Her heart was throbbing fast, but she could
not tell whether she awoke of herself or had
been aroused by some external cause.

"Who's there?" she cried, in a fright, as
she started up and looked about the room.

Exactly as she called she thought she
heard something fall—a heavy and muffled
sound. It might have been a room or two
away, it might have been nearer, but her
own voice made the sound uncertain. She
waited in alarm and listened, but for the
present all was again quiet.

Poor little Alice knew very well that she
was not herself, and her reason took comfort
from her consciousness of the excited state
of her nerves.

"What a fool I am!" she whispered, with
a sigh. "What a fool! Everything frightens
me now, I've grown such a coward. Oh!

Charlie, Charlie—oh, Ry, darling!—when will you come back to your poor wife—when shall this dreadful suspense be over and quiet come again?"

Then poor little Alice cried, after the manner of women, bitterly for a time, and then, as she used in all trouble, she prayed, and essayed to settle again to sleep. But hardly had she begun the attempt when it was terminated strangely.

Again she heard the same stealthy sound, as of something cutting or ripping. Again she cried "Hish, hish!" but with no effect. She fancied at the far corner of the room, about as high as she could easily reach, that she saw some glittering object. It might be a little bit of looking-glass pass slowly and tremulously along the wall, horizontally, and then with the same motion, in a straight line down the wall, glimmering faintly in the candle light. At the same time was a slight trembling of that part of the wall, a slight, wavy motion, and—could she believe her eyes ?—a portion of the wall seemed to yield silently, an unsuspected door slowly opened, and a tall figure wrapt in a flannel dress came in.

This figure crouched a little with its hand to its ear, and moved its head slowly round as if listening in all directions in turn. Then softly, with a large hand, it pushed back the door, which shut with a little snap, as if with a spring-lock.

Alice all this time was gazing upon the visitor, actually freezing with terror, and not knowing whether the apparition was that of a living person or not. The woollen-clothed figure, with large feet in stockings, and no shoes on, advanced, the fingers of one hand sliding gently along the wall. With an aspect fixed on the opposite end of the room, and the other hand a little raised in advance, it was such a fixed, listening look, and groping caution of motion as one might fancy in a person getting along a familiar room in the dark.

The feeling that she was not seen made Alice instinctively silent. She was almost breathless. The intruder passed on thus until she had reached the corner of the room, when she felt about for the door-case, and having got her hand upon it she quickly transferred it to the handle, which she turned, and tried the door two or three times.

Oh! what Alice would have given at this moment that she had not locked it, believing, as she now did, that the stranger would have passed out quietly from the room if this obstruction had not presented itself.

As if her life was concentrated in her eyes, Alice gazed still at this person, who paused for a few seconds, and lowering her head listened fixedly. Then very cautiously she with the tips of her fingers tried—was it to turn the key in the lock or to extricate it? At all events, she failed. She removed her hand, turned a little, stood still, and listened.

To Alice's horror her business in the room was plainly not over yet. The woman stood

erect, drawing a long breath, holding her
underlip slightly in her teeth, with just a
little nip. She turned her face toward the
bed, and for the first time Alice now quite
distinctly saw it—pale, seamed with small-
pox, blind. This large face was now turned
toward her, and the light of the candle,
screened by the curtain from Alice's eyes,
fell full upon its exaggerated and evil features.
The woman had drawn in a long, full breath,
as if coming to a resolution that needed some
nerve.

Whatever this woman had come into the
room for, Alice thought, with hope, that she
at all events, as she stood pallid and lowering
before her, with eyes white with cataract, and
brows contracted in malignant calculation,
knew nothing, as she undoubtedly saw nothing, of her.

Still as death sat Alice in her terror gazing
into the sightless face of this woman, little
more than two yards removed from her.

Suddenly this short space disappeared, and

with two swift steps and an outstretched hand she stood at the bedside and caught Alice's night-dress and drew her forcibly towards her. Alice as violently resisted. With a loud scream she drew back and the night-dress tore. But the tall woman instantly grasped her nearer the shoulder, and scrambling on the bed on her knees she dragged her down upon it, and almost instantly struck at her throat with a knife.

To make this blow she was compelled to withdraw one hand, and with a desperate spring, Alice evaded the stroke.

The whole thing was like a dream. The room seemed all a cloud. She could see nothing but the white figure that was still close, climbing swiftly over the bed, with one hand extended now and the knife in the other.

Not knowing how she got there, she was now standing with her back to the wall, in the further corner of the room, staring at the dreadful figure in a catalepsy of terror.

There was hardly a momentary pause. She was afraid to stir lest the slightest motion should betray her to the search of this woman. Had she, as she stood and listened sharply, heard her breathing?

With sudden decision, long light steps, and her hand laid to the wall, she glided swiftly toward her. With a gasp Alice awoke, as it were, from her nightmare, and, almost wild with terror, fled round the bed to the door. Hastening, jostling by the furniture, gliding, on the whole, very adroitly after her, her face strained with a horrible eagerness and fear, came the blind woman.

Alice tried to pull open the door. She had locked it herself, but in her agitation forgot.

Now she seized the key and tried to turn it, but the strong hand of the stranger in forcing it round a second time had twisted it so that it was caught in the lock and would not turn.

Alice felt as people feel in dreams, when

pursuit is urgent and some little obstruction
entangles flight and threatens to deliver the
fugitive into the hands of an implacable pursuer. A frantic pull and a twist or two of
the key in vain, and the hand of the pursuer
was all but upon her. Again she sprang
and scrambled across the bed, and it seemed
enraged by the delay and with a face sharp-
ening and darkening with insanity, the mur-
deress, guided by the sound, flung herself
after her; and now, through the room and
lobbies pealed shrieks of murder, as Alice
flew before the outstretched hand of the
beldame, who, balked of her prey, followed
with reckless fury, careless now against what
she struck or rushed, and clawing the air,
as it seemed, within an inch of Alice's
shoulder.

Unequal as it appeared, in this small pen,
the struggle to escape could not have lasted
very long. The old closet door, thinly
covered with paper, through which the sharp
knife had glided almost without noise, was

locked, and escape through it as hopeless as through the other door. Through the window she would have thrown herself, but it was fastened, and one moment's delay would have been death. Had a weapon been in her hand, had she thought of it in this extremity of terror, her softer instincts might have been reversed, and she might have turned on her pursuer and fought, as timid creatures have done, with the ferocity of despair, for her life. But the chance that might have so transformed her did not come. Flight was her one thought, and that ended suddenly, for tripping in the upturned carpet she fell helplessly to the floor. In a moment, with a gasp, her pursuer was kneeling by her side, with her hand in her dishevelled hair, and drawing herself close for those sure strokes of the knife with which she meant to mangle her.

As the eyes of the white owl glare through the leaves on the awaking bird, and its brain swims, and its little heart bounces into a gallop, seeing its most dreadful dream accomplished, escape impossible, its last hour come —then the talons of the spectre clutch its throat, and its short harmless life is out,—so might it have been with pretty Alice.

In that dreadful second of time all things that her eyes beheld looked strange, in a new reality—the room contracted, and familiar things were unlike themselves, and the certainty and nearness of that which she now knew—all her life before was but a dream to her—what an infidel, what a fool she had been,—*here* it was, and *now*—death.

The helpless yell that burst from her lips, as this dreadful woman shuffled nearer on her knees, was answered by a crash from the door burst in, and a cry from a manly voice— the door flew wide, and Alice saw her husband pale as death ; with a single savage blow he stretched her assailant on the floor,—in another moment Alice, wild with terror, half-fainting, was in his arms.

And—did he *strike* her ? Good God !—

had he struck her! How did she lie there bleeding? For a moment a dreadful remorse was bursting at his heart—he would have kneeled—he could have killed himself. Oh, manhood! Gratitude! Charity! Could he, even in a moment of frenzy, have struck down any creature so—that had ever stood to him in the relation of that love? What a rush of remembrances, and hell of compunction was there!—and for a rival! She the reckless, forlorn, guilty old love cast off, blasted with deformity and privation, and now this last fell atrocity! Alice was clinging to him, the words "darling, darling, my Ry, my saviour, my Ry," were in his ears, and he felt as if he hated Alice—hated her worse even than himself. He froze with horror and agony as he beheld the ineffaceable image of that white, blood-stained twitching face, with sightless eyes, and on the floor those straggling locks of changed, grizzled hair, that once were as black as a raven's wing to which he used to compare them.

Oh maddening picture of degradation and cruelty! To what had they both come at last?

But an iron necessity was upon him, and with an energy of hypocrisy, he said— "Alice, my treasure, my darling, you're safe, aren't you?"

"Oh, darling, yes," she gasped.

"Not here—you mustn't stay here—run down—she's mad—she's a mad woman—not here a moment."

Half stunned and dreamy with horror, Alice glided down the stairs, passing honest Tom who was stumbling up, half awake, but quite dressed excepting his coat.

"Run, Tom, help your master, for God's sake,—there's something dreadful," she said as she passed him with her trembling hands raised.

"Where, ma'am, may't be?" said Tom, pausing with a coolness that was dreadful, she thought.

"There, there, in his room, my room; go, for heaven's sake!"

Up ran Tom, making a glorious clatter with his hob-nails, and down ran Alice, and just at the foot of the stair she met Mildred Tarnley's tall slim figure. The old woman drew to the banister, and stood still, looking darkly and shrewdly at her.

"Oh! good Mildred—oh, Mrs. Tarnley, for God's sake don't leave me."

"And what's the row, ma'am, what is it?" asked Mrs. Tarnley, with her lean arm supporting the poor trembling young lady who clung to her.

"Oh, Mrs. Tarnley, take me with you—take me out—I can't stay in the house; take me away—into the woods—anywhere out of the house."

"Well, well, come down, come along," she said, more tenderly than was her wont, and watching her face hard from the corners of her eyes. She was convinced that the "old soldier" was the cause of these horrors.

"Put your arm over my shouther, ma'am; there—that's it—an' I'll put mine round you, if you don't think I'm making too bold. There now, you're more easy, I think."

And as they got on through the passage she asked—

"'Twas you that skritched, hey?"

"I? I dare say—did I?"

"Ay did ye, with a will, whoever skritched. Ye seen summat. What may ye have seen that frightened ye like that?"

"We'll talk by-and-by. I'm ill—I'm horribly ill. Come away."

"Come, then, if ye like best, ma'am," said Mildred Tarnley, leading her through the kitchen, and by the outer door into the open air, but she had hardly got a step into the yard when the young lady, holding her fast, stopped short in renewed terrors.

"Oh, Mildred, if she follows us, if she overtook us out here?"

"Hoot, ma'am, who are ye afeard on? Is it that crazy blind woman, or who?"

"Oh, Mildred, yes, it is she. Oh, Mildred, where shall we go, where can I hide myself? there's nowhere safe."

"Now you're just drivin' yourself distracted, you be. What for need ye fear her? She's crazy, I'll not deny, but she's blind too, and she can't follow ye here, if she was so minded. Why she couldn't cross the stile, nor follow ye through a spinnie. But see, ye've nout but yer dressin' gown over yer night clothes, and yer bare feet. Odd's I'll not go wi' ye—ye'll come back, and if ye must come abroad, ye'll get yer cloaks and your shoon."

"No, no, no, Mildred, I'll go as I am," cried the terrified lady, at the same time hurrying onward to the yard door.

"Well," said the old woman following, "wilful lass will ha' her way, but ye'll clap this ower your shouthers."

And she placed her own shawl on them, and together they passed into the lonely woodlands that, spreading upward from the glen of Carwell, embower the deep ravine that flanks the side of the Grange, and widening and deepening, enter the kindred shadows of the glen.

CHAPTER XIV.

A MESSENGER.

ALICE had not gone far when she was seized with a great shivering—the mediate process by which from high hysterical tension, nature brings down the nerves again to their accustomed tone.

The air was soft and still, and the faint gray of morning was already changing the darkness into its peculiar twilight.

"Ye'll be better presently, dear," said the old woman, with unaccustomed kindness. "There, there, ye'll be nothing the worse when a's done, and ye'll have a cup o' tea when ye come back."

Under the great old trees near the ivied wall which screens the court is a stone bench, and on this old Mildred was constrained to place her.

"There, there, there, rest a bit—rest a little bit. Hih! cryin'—well, cry if ye will; but ye'll ha' more to thank God than to cry for, if all be as I guess."

Alice cried on with convulsive sobs, starting every now and then, with a wild glance towards the yard gate, and grasping the old woman's arm. In a very few minutes this paroxysm subsided, and she wept quietly.

"'Twas you, ma'am, that cried out, I take it—hey? Frightened mayhap?"

"I was—yes—I—I'll wait a little, and tell you by-and-by—horribly—horribly."

"Ye needn't be afeerd here, and me beside ye, ma'am, and daylight a-comin', and I think I could gi'e a sharp guess at the matter. Ye saw her ladyship, I do suppose? The old soger, ma'am—ay, that's a sight might frighten a body—like a spirit a'most— a great white-faced, blind devil."

"Who is she? how did she come? She

tried to kill me. Oh! Mrs. Tarnley, I'm so terrified!"

And with these words Alice began to cry and tremble afresh.

"Hey! try to kill ye, did she? I'm glad o' that—right glad o't; 'twill rid us o' trouble, ma'am. But la! think o' that! And did she actually raise her hand to you!"

"Oh yes, Mrs. Tarnley—frightful. I'm saved by a miracle—I don't know how—the mercy of God only."

She was clinging to Mrs. Tarnley with a fast and trembling grasp.

"Zooks! the lass *is* frightened. Ye ha' seen sights to-night, young lady, ye'll remember. Young folk loves pleasure, and the world, and themselves ower well to trouble their heads about death or judgment, if the Lord in His mercy didn't shake 'em up from their dreams and their sins. 'Awake thou that sleepest,' says the Word, callin' loud in a drunken ear, at dead o' night, wi'

the house all round a-fire, as the parson says.
He's a good man, though I may ha' seen better,
in old days in Carwell pulpit.   So, 'tis all for
good, and in place o' crying ye should be
praisin' God for startlin' ye out o' your car-
nal sleep, and makin' ye think o' him, and
see yourself as ye are, and not according to
the flatteries o' your husband and your own
vanity.   Ye'll pardon me, but truth is truth,
and God's truth first of all ; and who'll tell it
ye if them as is within hearin' won't open
their lips, and I don't see that Mr. Charles
troubles his head much about the matter."

"He is so noble, and always my guardian
angel.   Oh, Mrs. Tarnley, to-night I must
have perished if it had not been for him ; he
is always my best friend, and so unselfish
and noble."

"Well that's good," said Mildred Tarnley,
coldly.   "But I'm thinkin' something ought
to be done wi' that catamountain in there,
and strike while the iron's hot, and they'll
never drive home that nail ye'll find—more

like to go off when all's done wi' her pocket full o' money. 'Tis a sin, while so many an honest soul wants, and I'll take that just into my own old hands, I'm thinkin', and sarve her out as she would better women."

"Isn't she mad, Mrs. Tarnley?" asked Alice.

"And if she's mad, to the madhouse wi' her, an' if she's not, where's the gallows high enough for her, the dangerous harridan? For, one way or t'other, the fiend's in her, and the sooner judgment overtakes her, and she's in her coffin, the sooner the devil's laid, and the better for honest folk."

"If she is mad, it accounts for every-thing; but I feel as if I never could enter that house again; and oh! Mrs. Tarnley, you *mustn't* leave me. Oh, heavens! what's that?"

It was no great matter—Mrs. Tarnley had got up, for the yard-door had opened and some one passed out and looked round.

It was the girl, Lilly Dogger, who stood

there looking about her under the canopy of tall trees.

"Hoot, ma'm, 'tis only the child Lilly Dogger—and well pleased I am, for I was thinkin' this minute how I could get her to me quietly. Here, Lilly—come here, ye goose-cap—d'ye see me?"

So, closing the door behind her, the girl approached with eyes very wide, and a wonderfully solemn countenance. She had been roused and scared by the sounds which had alarmed the house, huddled on her clothes, and seeing Mrs. Tarnley's figure cross the window, had followed in a tremor.

Mrs. Tarnley walked a few steps towards her, and beckoning with her lean finger, the girl drew near.

"Ye'll have to go over Cressley Common, girl, to Wykeford. Ye know Wykeford?"

"Yes, please 'm."

"Well, ye must go through the village, and call up Mark Topham. Ye know Mark Topham's house with the green door, by the bridge-end ?"

"Yes please, Mrs. Tarnley, ma'am."

"And say he'll be wanted down here at the Grange—for *murder* mind—and go ye on to Mr. Rodney at t'other side o' the river. Squire Rodney of Wrydell. Ye know that house, too ?"

"Yes, 'em," said the girl, with eyes momentarily distending, and face of blanker consternation.

"And ye'll tell Mr. Rodney there's been bad work down here, and murder all but done, and say ye've told Mark Topham, the constable, and that it is hoped he'll come over himself to make out the writin's and send away the prisoner as should go. We being chiefly women here, and having to keep Tom Clinton at home to mind the prisoner—ye understand—and keep all safe, having little other protection. Now run in, lass, and clap your bonnet on, and away wi' ye ; and get ye there as fast as your legs will carry ye, and take your time comin' back; and ye may get a lift, for they'll not be walkin', and you're like to get your bit o' breakfast down at Wrydell; but if ye shouln't, here's tuppence, and buy yourself a good bit o' bread in the town. Now, ye understand?"

"Yes, 'm, please."

"And ye'll not be makin' mistakes, mind?"

"No, ma'am."

"Then do as I bid ye, and off ye go," said Mrs. Tarnley, despatching her with a peremptory gesture.

So with a quaking heart, not knowing what dangers might still be lurking there, Lilly Dogger ran into the yard on her way to her bonnet, and peeped through the kitchen window, but saw nothing there in the pale gray light but "still life."

With a timid finger she lifted the latch, and stole into the familiar passage as if she were exploring a haunted house. She had quaked in her bed as thin and far away the shrill sounds of terror had penetrated through

walls and passages to her bed-room. She
had murmured " Lord bless us ! " at intervals, and listened, chilled with a sense of
danger—associated in her imagination with
the stranger who had visited her room and
frighted away her slumbers. And she had
jumped out of bed, and thrown on her clothes
in panic, blessed herself, and pinned and
tied strings, and listened, and blessed herself
again ; and seeing Mrs. Tarnley cross the
window accompanied by some one else whom
she did not then recognise, and fearing to
remain thus deserted in the house more than
the risk of being blown up by Mrs. Tarnley,
she had followed that grim protectress.

Now, as on tiptoe she recrossed the kitchen
with her straw bonnet in her hand she heard
on a sudden cries of fury, and words, as doors
opened and shut, reached her that excited
her horror and piqued her curiosity.

She hastened, however, to leave the house,
and again approached and passed by the
lady and Mildred Tarnley, having tied her

bonnet under her chin, and obeying Mildred's impatient beckon, and—

"Run, lass, run. Stir your stumps, will ye?"

She started at a pace that promised soon to see her across Cressley Common.

Old Mildred saw this with comfort. She knew that broad-shouldered, brown-eyed lass for a shrewd and accurate messenger, and seeing how dangerous and complicated things were growing, she was glad that fortune had opened so short and sharp a way of getting rid of the troubler of their peace.

"Come in, ma'am, ye'll catch your death o' cold here. All's quiet by this time, and I'll make the kitchen safe against the world; and Mr. Charles is in the house, and Tom Clinton up, and all safe—and who cares a rush for that blind old cat? Not I for one. She'll come no nonsense over Mildred Tarnley in her own kitchen, while there's a poker to rap her ower the pate. Hoot! one old blind limmer; I'd tackle six o' her sort, old as I am, and tumble 'em one after t'other into the Brawl. Never ye trouble your head about that, ma'am, and I'll bolt the door on the passage, and the scullery door likewise, and lock 'em if ye like; and we'll get down old Dulcibella to sit wi' ye, and ye'll be a deal less like to see that beast in the kitchen than here. There's Miss Crane," by which title she indicated old Dulcibella, "a lookin' out o' her window. Ho! Miss Crane—will ye please, Miss Crane, come down and stay a bit wi' your mistress?"

"Thank God!—is she down there?" exclaimed she.

"Come down, ma'am, please; she's quite well, and she'll be glad to see ye."

Old Dulcibella's head disappeared from the window promptly.

"Now, ma'am, she'll be down, and when she comes—for ye'd like to ha' some one by ye—I'll go in and make the kitchen door fast."

"And won't you search it well, Mrs. Tarn-

ley, and the inner room, that we may be
certain no one is hid there ? Pray do—may
I rely on you—won't you promise ?"

"There's nothin' there, that I promise ye."

"But, oh ! pray do," urged Alice.

"I will, ma'am, just to quiet ye. Ye need
not fear, I'll leave her no chance, and she'll
soon be safe enough, she shall—safe enough
when she gets on her doublet of stone ; and
don't ye be frightenin' yourself for nothin'—
just keep yourself quiet, for there is nothing
to fear, and if ye will keep yourself in a fever
for nothin' ye'll be just making food for
worms, mark my words."

As she spoke old Dulcibella appeared, and
with a face of deep concern waddled as fast
as she could toward her young mistress,
raising her hands and eyes from time to
time as she approached.

As she drew nearer she made a solemn
thanksgiving, and—

"Oh! my child, my child, thank God
you're well. I was a'most ready to drop in

a swound when I came into your room, just now, everything knocked topsy-turvey, and a door cut in the wall, and all in a litter, I couldn't know where I was, and some one a bleedin' all across the floor, and one of the big, green-handled knives on the floor—Lord a' mercy on us—with the blade bent and blood about it. I never was so frightened. I thought my senses was a leavin' me, and I couldn't tell what I might see next, and I ready to drop down on the floor wi' fright. My darling child—my precious—Lord love it, and here it was, barefooted, and but half clad, and—come in ye must, dear, 'tis enough to kill ye."

"I can scarcely remember anything, Dulcibella, only one thing—oh! I'm so terrified."

"Come in, darling, you'll lose your life if you stay here as you are, and what was it, dear, and who did you see?"

"A woman—that dreadful blind woman, who came in at the new door; I never saw her before."

"Well, *dear!* Oh, Miss Alice, darling, I couldn't a' believed, and thank God you're safe after all; that's she I heard a screechin' as strong as a dozen—and frightful words, as well as I could hear, to come from any woman's lips. Lord help us."

"Where is she now?"

"Somewhere in the front of the house, darlin', screechin' and laughin' I thought, but heaven only knows."

"She's mad, Mrs. Tarnley says, and Mr. Fairfield said so too. Master Charles is come —my darling Ry. Oh! Dulcibella, how grateful I should be. What could I have done if he hadn't?"

So Dulcibella persuaded her to come into the yard, and so, through the scullery door, at which Mildred stood, having secured all other access to the kitchen. So in she came, awfully frightened to find herself again in the house, but was not her husband there, and help at hand, and the doors secured?

CHAPTER XV.

HER husband was at hand—that is to say, under the same roof, and at that moment in the room in which the blind woman was now sitting, bleeding from her head and hand, and smiling as she talked, with the false light of a malignant irony.

"So, husband and wife are met again! And what have you to say after so long a time?"

"I've nothing to say. Let my deeds speak. I've given you year by year fully half my income."

She laughed scornfully, and exclaimed merely—

"Magnificent man!"

"Miserable pittance it is, but the more

miserable, the harder the sacrifice for me.   I
don't say I have been able to do much ; but
I have done more than my means warrant,
and I don't understand what you propose to
yourself by laying yourself out to torment
and embarrass me.   What the devil do you
follow me about for ?   Do you think I'm
fool enough to be bullied ? "

" A fine question from Charles Vairfield of
Wyvern to his wife ! " she observed with a
pallid simper.

" Wife and husband are terms very easily
pronounced," said he.

" And relations very easily made," she re-
joined.

He was leaning with his shoulder against
the high mantelpiece, and looking upon her
with a countenance in which you might have
seen disdain and fear mingling with something of compunction.

" Relations very easily made, and still
more easily affected," he replied.   " Come,
Bertha, there is no use in quarrelling over

points of law. Past is past, as Leonora says. If I have wronged you in anything I am sorry. I've tried to make amends; and though many a fellow would have been tired out long ago, I continue to give you proofs that I am not."

"That is a sort of benevolence," she said, in her own language, "which may as well be voluntary, for, if it be not, the magistrates will compel it."

"The magistrates are neither fools nor tyrants. You'll make nothing of the magistrates. You have no rights, and you know it."

"An odd country where a wife has no rights."

"Come, Bertha, there is no use in picking a quarrel. While you take me quietly you have your share, and a good deal more. You used to be reasonable."

"A reasonable wife, I suppose, gives up her position, her character, her prospects, whenever it answers her husband to sacrifice these trifles for his villanous pleasures. Your English wives must be meek souls indeed if they like it. I don't hear they are such lambs though."

"I'm not going to argue law points, as I said before. Lawyers are the proper persons to do that. You used to be reasonable, Bertha—where's the good in pushing things to extremes?"

"What a gentle creature you are," she laughed, "and how persuasive!"

"I'm a quiet fellow enough, I believe, as men go, but I'm not persuasive, and I know it. I wish I were."

"Those whom you have persuaded once are not likely to be persuaded again. Your persuasions are not always lucky. Are they?"

"You want to quarrel about everything. You want to leave no possible point of agreement."

"Things are at a bad pass when husband and wife are so."

Charles looked at her angrily for a moment, and then down to the floor, and he whistled a few bars of a tune.

"What do you whistle for?" she demanded.

"Come, Bertha, don't be foolish."

"You were once a gentleman. It is a blackguard who whistles in reply to a lady's words," she said, on a sudden stretching out her hand tremulously, as if in search of some one to grasp.

"Well, don't mind. Stick to one thing at a time. For God's sake say what you want, and have done with it."

"You must acknowledge me before the world for your wife," she answered with resolute serenity, and raising her face, and shutting her mouth she sniffed defiantly through her distended nostrils.

"Come, come, Bertha, what good on earth could come of that?"

"Little to you, perhaps."

"And none to you."

She laughed savagely. "That lie won't do."

"Bertha, Bertha, we may hate one another if you will. But is it not as well to try whether we can agree upon anything. Let us just for the present talk intelligibly."

"You tried to murder me, you arch-villain."

"Nonsense," said he, turning pale, "how can you talk so—how can you? Could I help interposing? You may well be thankful that I did."

"You tried to murder me," she screamed.

"You know that's false. I took the knife from your hand, and by doing so I saved two lives. It was you—not I—who hurt your hand."

"You villain, you damned villain, I wish I could kill you dead."

"All the worse for you, Bertha."

"I wish you were dead and cold in your bed, and my hand on your face to be sure of it."

"Now you're growing angry again. I thought we had done with storm and hysterics for a little, and could talk, and perhaps agree upon something, or at all events not waste our few minutes in violence."

"Violence!—you wretch, who began it?"

"What can you mean, Bertha?"

"You've married that woman. O I know it all—I your lawful wife living. I'll have you transported, double-dyed villain."

"Where's the good of screaming all this at the top of your voice?" he said, at last growing angry. "You wish you could kill me? I almost wish you could. I've been only too good to you, and allowed you to trouble me too long."

"Ha, ha!—you'd like to put me out of the way?"

"You'll do that for yourself. Can't you wait, can't you listen, can't you have common reason, just for one moment? What do you want, what do you wish? Do you want every farthing I possess on earth, and to leave me nothing ? "

" I'm your wife, and I'll have my rights."

" Now listen to me, that's a question I need not discuss, because you already know what I believe on the subject."

" You know what your brother Harry thinks."

" I know what it is his interest to think."

" You daren't say that if he were here, you coward."

" And I don't care a farthing what he thinks."

" Ha, ha, ha ! "

" But if it had been fifty times over, what it never was, a marriage, your own conduct, long ago, would have dissolved it."

" And you allow you have married that woman ? "

" I shan't talk to you about it ; how I shall act, or may act, or *have* acted is my own affair, and rely upon it I'll do nothing on the assumption that I ever was married to you."

Up stood the tall woman, with hands extended toward him, wide open, with a slightly groping motion as if opening a curtain ; not a word did she say, but her sightless eyes, which stared full at him, were quivering with that nervous tremor which is so unpleasant to see.

She drew breath two or three times at intervals, long and deep, almost a sob, and then without speaking or moving more she sat down, looking awfully white and wicked.

For a time the old soldier had lost the thread of her discourse. Charles heard a step not very far off. He thought his unreasonable Bertha was about to have a fit, and opening the door he called lustily to Mildred.

It *was* Mrs. Tarnley.

"Will you get her some water, or whatever she ought to have, I think she is ill, and pray be quick."

With a dark prying look Mildred glanced from one to the other.

"It's in a mad-house and not here the like of her should be, wi' them fits and frenzies," she muttered as she applied herself to the resuscitation of the Dutchwoman.

On her toilet was a little group of bottles labelled "Sal-volatile," "Asafœtida," "Valerian."

"I don't know which is the right one, but this can't be far wrong," she remarked, selecting the sal-volatile, and dropping some into the water.

"La! so it was a sort o' fit. See how stiff she was. Lor' bless us, I do wish she was under a mad doctor. See how her feet's stuck out, and her thumbs tight shut in her fists, and her teeth set," and old Mildred applied the sal-volatile phial to the patient's nostrils, and gradually got her into a drowsy, yawning state, in which she seemed to care and comprehend little or nothing of where she was or what had befallen her.

"Tell her I stayed till I saw her better, if she asks, and that I'm coming back again. She says she is hurt."

"So much the better," said Mildred; "that will keep her from prowling about the house like a cat or a ghost, as she did, all night, and no good came of it."

"And will you look to her wrist: she cut it last night, and it is very clumsily tied up, and I'll come again, tell her."

So, with a bewildered brain and a direful load at his heart, he left the room.

Where was Alice, he thought. He went downstairs and up again by the back staircase to their room, and there found the wreck and disorder of the odious scene he had witnessed, still undisturbed, and looking somehow more shocking in the sober light of morning.

From this sickening record of the occurrences of last night he turned for a moment to the window, and looked out on the tranquil and sylvan solitudes, and then back again upon the disorder which had so nearly marked a scene of murder.

"How do I keep my reason?" thought he; "is there in England so miserable a man? Why should not I end it?"

Between the room where he stood and the angle of that bedroom in which at that moment was the wretch who agitated every hour of his existence with dismay, there intervened but eight-and-twenty feet, in that polyhedric and irregular old house. If he had but one· tithe of her wickedness he had but to take up that poker, strike through, and brain her as she sat there.

Why was he not a little more or a little less wicked? If the latter, he might never have been in his present fix. If the other, he might find a short way out of the thicket— "hew his way out with a bloody axe"—and none but those whose secrecy he might rely on be the wiser!

Avaunt, horrible shadows! Such beckoning phantoms from the abyss were not tempters, but simply terrors. No, he was far more likely to load a pistol, put the muzzle in his mouth, and blow his harrassed brains out.

CHAPTER XVI.

AN ABDUCTION.

So far as a man not very resolute can be said to have made up his mind to anything, Charles Fairfield had quite made up his, driven thus fairly into a corner, to fight his battle now, and decisively. He would hold no terms and offer no compromise. Let her do her worst. She had found out his secret. Oh! brother Harry, had *you* played him false? And she had quoted *your* opinion against him. Had you been inflaming this insane enemy with an impracticable confidence?

Well, no matter, now; all the better, perhaps. There was already an end of concealment between that enemy and himself, and soon would be of suspense.

" God help me ! at the eve of what an abyss I stand. That wretched woman, poor as she is, and nearly mad, in a place like London she'll be certain to find lawyers only too glad to take up her case, and force me to a trial—first, a trial to prove a marriage and make costs of me, and then, Heaven knows what more ; and the publicity, and the miserable uncertainty ; and Alice, poor little Alice. Merciful Heaven ! what had she done to merit this long agony and possible ruin ? "

He peeped into the dining-room as he passed, but all was there as he had left it. Alice had not been in it. So at the kitchen door he knocked.

" Who's there ? Is anyone there ? "

Encouraged by his voice old Dulcibella answered from within. The door was opened, and he entered.

A few moments' silence, except for Alice's murmured and sobbing welcome, a trembling, close embrace, and he said, with a gentle look, in a faint tone—

" Alice, darling, I have no good news to tell. Everything has gone wrong with me, and we must leave this. Let Dulcibella go up and get such things as are necessary to take with you ; but, Dulcibella, mind you tell nobody your mistress is leaving this. And, Alice, you'll come with me. We'll go where they can neither follow nor trace us ; and let fate do its worst. We may be happier yet in our exile than ever we were at home. And when they have banished me they have done their worst."

His tenderness for Alice, frozen for a time, had returned. As she clung to him, her large, soft gray eyes looking up in his face so piteously moved him. He had intended a different sort of speech—colder, dryer—and under the spell of that look had come this sudden gush of a better feeling— the fond clasp of his arm, and the hurried kiss he pressed upon her cheek.

"I said, Alice, happier, *happier*, darling, a

thousandfold. For the present I speak in riddles. You have seen how miserable I am. I'll tell you everything by-and-by. A conspiracy, I do believe, an unnatural conspiracy, that has worn out my miserable brain and spirits, and harassed me to death. I'll tell you all time enough, and you'll say it is a miracle I have borne it as I do. Don't look so frightened, you poor little thing. We are perfectly safe ; I'm in no real danger, but harassed incessantly—only harassed, and that, thank God, shall end."

He kissed her again very tenderly, and again ; and he said—

" You and Dulcibella shall go on. Clinton will drive you to Hatherton, and there you'll get horses and post on to Cranswell, and I will overtake you there. I must go now and give him his directions, and I may as well leave you this note. I wrote it yesterday. You must have some money—there is some in it, and the names of the places, and we'll be there to-night. And what is it, darling ?

You look as if you wished to ask me something."

"I—I was going to ask—but I thought perhaps I ought not until you can tell me everything—but you spoke of a conspiracy, and I was going to ask whether that dreadful woman who got into my room has anything to do with it."

"Nonsense, child, that is a miserable mad woman ;" he laughed dismally. "Just wait a little, and you shall know all I know myself."

"She's not to stay here, I mean, of course, if anything should prevent our leaving this to-day."

"Why should you fancy that ?" he asked, a little enigmatically.

"Mrs. Tarnley said she was going to the madhouse."

"We'll see time enough, you shall see her no more," he said, and away he went, and she saw him pass by the window and out of the yard. And now she had leisure to think how ill he was looking, or rather to remember how it had struck her when he had appeared at the door. Yes, indeed, worn out and harassed to death. Thank God, he was now to escape from that misery, and to secure the repose which it was only too obvious he needed.

Dulcibella returned with such things as she thought indispensable, and she and her mistress were soon in more animated discussion than they had engaged in since the scenes of the past night.

Charles Fairfield had to make a call at farmer Chubb's to persuade him to lend his horse, about which he made a difficulty. It was not far up the glen towards Church Carwell, but when he came back he found the Grange again in a new confusion.

When Charles Fairfield, ascending the steep and narrow road which under tall trees darkly mounts from the Glen of Carwell to the plateau under the grey walls of the Grange, had reached that sylvan platform,

he saw there, looking in the direction of
Cressley Common, in that dim, religious
light, Tom Clinton, in his fustian jacket,
scratching his head and looking, it seemed,
with interest, after some receding object.   A
little behind him, similarly engrossed, stood
old Mildred Tarnley, with her hand above
her eyes, though there was little need of
artificial shade in that solemn grove, and
again, a little to her rear, peeped broad-
shouldered Lilly Dogger, standing close to the
threshold of the yard door.

Tom Clinton was first to turn about, and
sauntering slowly toward the house, he spoke
something to Mrs. Tarnley, who, waiting till
he reached her, turned about in the same
direction, and talking gravely, and looking
over their shoulders, as people sometimes do
in the direction in which a runaway horse
has disappeared, they came to a standstill at
the door, under the great ash-tree, whose
columnar stem is mantled with thick ivy, and
there again looking back, the little girl

leaning and listening, unheeded, against the door-post, the group remained in conference.

Had Charles Fairfield been in his usual state of mind his curiosity would have been piqued by an appearance of activity so unusual in his drowsy household. As it was, he cared not, but approached, looking down upon the road with his hands in his pockets listlessly.

Mrs. Tarnley whispered something to Tom and jogged him in the ribs, looking all the time at the approaching figure of Charles Fairfield.

The master of the Grange approached, looked up, and saw Tom standing near, with the air of one who had something to say. Mrs. Tarnley had drawn back, a little doubtful possibly, of the effect on his nerves.

"Well, Tom Chubbs will lend the horse," said Charles. "We'll go round to the stable, I've a word to say."

Tom touched his hat, still looking in his

face with an inquiring and ominous expression.

"Do you want to say anything particular, Tom?" asked his master, with a sudden foreboding of some new ill.

"Nothing, sir, but Squire Rodney of Wrydell, has come over from Wykeford."

"He's here—is he?" asked Charles, paler on a sudden.

"He's gone, sir, please."

"Gone, is he? Well, well, there's not much in that."

"'Twas only, sir, that he brought two men wi' him."

"Do you mean?—you don't mean—what men did he bring?"

"Well, they was constable folk, I believe, they must a' bin, for they made an arrest."

"A *what,* do you mean?"

"He made out a writin', and he 'ad me in, and questioned me, but I'd nout to tell, sir, and he asked where you was, and I told him, as you ordered I was to say, you was gone, and he took the mistress's her story, and made her make oath on't, and the same wi' the others—Mrs. Tarnley, and the little girl, and the blind woman, she be took up for murder, or I don't know for what, only he said he could not take no bail for her, so they made her sure, and has took her off, I do suppose, to Wykeford pris'n."

"Of course, that's right, I suppose, all right, eh?" Charles looked as if he was going to drop to the earth, so leaden was his hue, and so meaningless the stare with which he looked in Tom's face.

"But—but—who sent for him? I didn't. D—— you, who sent for him? 'Twasn't I. And—and who's master here? Who the devil sent for that meddling rascal from Wykeford?"

Charles's voice had risen to a roar as he shook Tom furiously by the collar.

Springing back a bit, Tom answered, with his hand grasping his collar where the squire had just clutched him.

"I don't know, I didn't, and I don't believe no one did. It's a smart run from here across the common. I don't believe no one sent from the Grange—I'm sure no one went from this—not a bit, not a toe, not a soul, I'm sure and certain."

"What's this, what's this, what the devil's all this, Tom?" said the squire, stamping, and shaking his fist in the air, like a man distracted.

"Why did you let her go—why did you let them take her—d—— you? I've a mind to pitch you over that cliff and smash you."

"Well, sir," said Tom, making another step or two back, and himself pale and stern now, with his open hand raised, partly in deprecation, "where's the good o' blamin' me? what could I do wi' the law again me, and how could I tell what you'd think, and *'twarn't* no one from this sent for him, not one, but news travels a-pace, and who's he can stop it?—not me, nor *you*," said Tom, sturdily, " and he just come over of his own head, and nabbed her."

" My God ! It's done. I thought you would not have allowed me to be trampled on, and the place insulted ; I took ye for a man, Tom. Where's my horse—by heaven, I'll have him. I'll make it a day's work he'll remember. That d—— Rodney, coming down to my house with his catchpoles, to pay off old scores, and insult me."

With his fist clenched and raised, Charles Fairfield ran furiously round to the stable yard, followed cautiously by Tom Clinton.

CHAPTER XVII.

PURSUIT.

HAVING her own misgivings as to the temper in which her master would take this *coup* of the arrest, Mildred Tarnley prudently kept her own counsel, and retreated nearly to the kitchen door, while the *éclaircissement* took place outside. Popping in and out to see what would come of it, old Mildred affected to be busy about her mops and tubs. After a time, in came Tom, looking sulky and hot.

"Is he comin' this way?" asked Mildred.

"Not him," answered Tom.

"Where is he?"

"'Twixt this and Wykeford," he answered, "across the common he's ridin'."

"To Wykeford, hey?"

"To Wykeford, every foot, if he don't run him down on the way ; and when they meet —him and Squire Rodney—'twill be hot and shrewd work between them, I tell ye. I'd a rid wi' him myself if there was a beast to carry me, for three agin one is too long odds."

"Ye don't mean to tell *me !*" exclaimed Mildred, planting her mop perpendicularly on the ground, and leaning immovably on this sceptre.

"Tell ye what ?"

"There's goin' to be rough work like that on the head o't ?"

"Hot blood, ma'am. Ye know the Fairfields. They folk don't stand long jawin'. It's like when the blood's up the hand's up too."

"And what's he to fight for—not that blind beldame, sure ?"

"I want my mug o' beer," said Tom, turning the conversation.

"Yes, sure," she said, "yes, ye shall have

it. But what for should master Charles go to wry words wi' Squire Rodney, and what for should there be blows and blood spillin' between 'em? Nonsense!"

"I can't help 'em. I'd lend master a hand if I could. Squire Rodney's no fool neither —'twill e'en be fight dog, fight bear—and there's two stout lads wi' him will make short work o't."

"Ye don't think he's like to be hurt, do ye?"

"Well, ye know, they say fightin' dogs comes haltin' home. He's as strong as two, that's all, and has a good nag under him. Now gi'e me my beer."

"'Twon't be nothin', Tom, don't you think, Tom? It won't come to nothin'?"

"If he comes up wi' them 'twill be an up-and-down fight, I take it. 'Twas an unlucky maggot bit him."

"Bit who?"

"What but the Divil brought Squire Rodney over here?"

" Who knows ? " answered the dame, fumbling in her pocket for the key of the beercellar—" I'm goin' to fetch your beer, Tom."

And away she went, and in a minute returned with his draught of beer.

" And I think," she said, setting it down before him, " 'twas well done, taking that beast to her right place, do it who might. She's just a bedlam Bess—clean out o' her wits wi' wickedness—mad wi' drink and them fits she has. We knows here what she is, and bloody work she'd a made last night wi' that poor young lady, that'll never be the same again—the old limb—and master himself, though he's angered a bit because Justice Rodney did not ask his leave to catch a murderer, if ye please, down here at the Grange ! "

" There's more in it, mayhap, than just that," said Tom, blowing the froth off his beer.

" To come down here without with your leave or by your leave, to squat in the

Grange here like gipsey would on Cressley
Common, as tho' she was lady of all—to hurt
who she pleased, and live as she liked. More
in't than that, ye say, what more ? "

"Hoot, how should I know ? Mayhap she
thinks she's as good a right as another to
a bit and a welcome down here."

"She was here before—years enough gone
now, and long enough she stayed, and cost
a pretty penny, too, I warrant you. Them
was more tired of her than me—guest ever,
welcome never, they say. She was a play-
actor, or something, long ago—a great idle
huzzy, never would earn a honest penny, nor
do nothing useful, all her days."

"Ay, Joan reels ill and winds worse, and
de'il a stomach she has to spin—that'll be
the way wi' her, I swear—ha, ha, ha. She'll
not be growin' richer, I warrant—left in the
mud and found in the mire—they folk knows
nout o' thrift, and small luck and less good
about 'em."

"If ye heard her talk, Tom, ye'd soon

know what sort she is, always cravin'—she would not leave a body a shillin' if she could help it."

"Ay, I warrant, women, priests, and poultry have never enough," said Tom. "I know nout about her, nor who she's a lookin' after here, but she's safe enough now I take it; and bloody folks, they say, digs their own graves. But as I said, I knows nout about her, and I say nout, and he that judges as he runs may owertake repentance."

"'Tis easy judgin' here, I'm thinkin'. Killin' and murder's near akin, and when Mr. Charles cools a bit, he'll thank Squire Rodney for riddin' his house of that blind serpent. 'Tis somethin' to be so near losing his wife. So sure as your hand's on that mug it would a' bin done while the cat's lickin' her ear if he had not bounced in on the minute, and once dead, dead as Adam."

"Who loseth his wife and sixpence hath lost a tester, they do say," answered Tom, with a laugh.

"None but a born beast would say so!" said Mildred Tarnley, with a swarthy flush, and striking her hand sternly on the table.

"Well, 'tis only a sayin', ye know, and no new one neither," said Tom, wiping his mouth with his sleeve, and standing up. "But the mistress is a pretty lady, and a kind—and a gentle-born as all may see, and I'd give or take a shrewd blow or two, or harm should happen her."

"Ye'd be no man else, Tom, and I don't doubt ye. Little thought I last night what was in her head, the sly villain, when I left her back again in her bed, and the cross door shut and locked. Lord a' mercy on us! To think how the fiend works wi' his own— smooth and sly sometimes, as if butter would not melt in her mouth."

"'Tis an old sayin'—

"'When the cat winketh,
Little wots mouse what the cat thinketh.'"

said Tom, with a grin and a wag of his head.

"She was neither sleek, nor soft, nor sly

for that matter, when I saw her. I thought she'd a' had her claws in my chops; such a catamaran I never did see."

"And how's the young lady?" asked Tom, clapping his greasy hat on his head.

"Hey! dear! I'm glad ye asked," exclaimed the old woman—"easier she'll be, no doubt, now *that* devil's gone. But, dearie me! all's in a jumble till Master Charles comes back, for she'll not know, poor thing, what she's to do till he talks wi' her—now all's changed."

And Mildred trotted off to see for herself, and to hear what the young lady might have to say.

CHAPTER XVIII.

DAY—TWILIGHT—DARKNESS.

In their homely sitting-room, with old Dulcibella in friendly attendance, Mildred Tarnley found Alice. It is not always that a dreadful impression makes itself immediately manifest. Nature rallies all her forces at first to meet the danger. A certain excitement of resistance sustains the system through a crisis of horror, and often for a long time after; and it is not until this extraordinary muster of the vital forces begins to dissolve and subside that the shattered condition of the normal powers begins to declare itself.

The scene which had just occurred was a dreadful ordeal for Alice. To recount, and with effort and minuteness, to gather into

order the terrific incidents of the night pre-
ceding, relate them bit by bit to the magistrate as he wrote them down, make oath to
their truth as the basis of a public prosecu-
tion, and most dreadful—the having to see
and identify the spectre who had murder-
ously assailed her on the night before.

Every step affrighted her, the shadow of a
moving branch upon the wall chilled her
with terror ; the voices of people who spoke
seemed to pierce the naked nerve of her ear,
and to sing through her head ; even for a
moment faces, kind and familiar, seemed to
flicker or darken with direful meanings alien
from their natures.

In this nervous condition old Mildred
found her.

" I come, ma'am, to know what you'd wish
to be done," said she, standing at the door
with her usual grim little courtesy.

" I don't quite understand—done about
what ? " inquired she.

" I mean, ma'am, Tom said you asked him

to be ready to drive you from here ; but as
master ha'n't come back, and things is
changed a bit here, I thought ye might
wish to make a change, mayhap."

"Oh, oh! thank you, Mrs. Tarnley ; I
forgot, I've been so frightened. Oh, Mrs.
Tarnley, I wish I could cry—I'd be so much
better, I'm sure, if I could cry—I feel my
throat so odd and my head so confused—
it seems so many days. If I could think of
anything to make me cry."

Mildred looked at her from the corners of
her eyes darkly, as if with a hard heart, but
I think she pitied her.

"That blind woman's gone, the beast—I'm
glad she's away ; and you'll be the better o'
that, ma'am, I'm thinkin'. I was afeard o'
her a'most myself ever since last night ; and
Master Charles is gone, too, but he'll be back
soon."

"He'll come *to-day?*" she asked, in consternation.

"To-day, of course, ma'am—in an hour or

less, I do suppose ; and it would not be well done, I'm thinkin', ma'am, for you to leave the Grange, till you see him again, for it's like enough he'll a' changed his plans."

" I was thinking so myself. I'd rather wait here to see him—he had so much to distract him that he may easily think differently by this time. I'm glad, Mrs. Tarnley, you think so, for now I feel confident I may wait for his return—I think I ought to wait—and thank you, Mrs. Tarnley, for advising me in the midst of my distractions."

" I just speak my mind, ma'am, and counsel's no command, as they say ; and I never liked meddlers ; and don't love to burn my fingers in other people's brewes : so ye'll please to mind, ma'am, 'tis for your own ear I speak, and your own wit will judge ; and I wouldn't have Master Charles looking askew, nor like to be shent by him for what's kindly meant to you—not that I owe much kindness nowhere, for since I could scour a platter I ever gave work for wage. So ye'll please not tell Master Charles I counselled ye aught in the matter."

"Certainly, Mrs. Tarnley, just as you wish."

"Would you please wish anything to eat, ma'am?" inquired Mildred, relapsing into her dry, official manner.

"Nothing, Mildred—no, thanks."

"Ye'll lose heart, miss, if ye don't eat—ye must eat."

"Thanks, Mildred, by-and-by, perhaps."

Mrs. Tarnley, like many worthy people, regarded eating as a simply mechanical process, and wondered why people affected a difficulty about it under any circumstances. Somewhat hard of heart, and with nerves of wire, she had no idea that a sufficient shock might rob one not only of appetite, but positively of the power of eating for days.

Alone, for one moment, Alice could not endure to be—haunted unintermittingly by the vague but intense dread of a return of the woman who had so nearly succeeded in murdering her, and with nerves shattered in that indescribable degree which even a strong man experiences for a long time after a murder has been attempted upon him perfidiously and by a surprise. The worst panic comes after an interval of many hours.

As the day waned, more miserably nervous she became, and more defined her terror of the Dutchwoman's return. That straggling old house, with no less than four doors of entrance, favoured the alarms of her imagination. Often she thought of her kind old kinswoman, Lady Wyndale, and her proffered asylum at her snug house at Oulton.

But that was a momentary picture—no more. Miserable as she was at the Grange, until she had seen her husband, learned his plans, and knew what his wishes were, that loyal little wife could not dream of going to Oulton.

She remained there as the shades of evening darkened over the steep roof and solemn trees of Carwell Grange, and more and-more grew the horror that deepened with darkness, and was aggravated and distracted by the continued absence of her husband.

In the sitting-room she stood, listening, with a beating heart. Every sound, which at another time would have been unheard, now thrilled her with hope or terror.

Old Dulcibella in the room was also frightened—more a great deal than she could account for. And even Mildred Tarnley—that hard and grim old lady—was touched by the influence of that contagious fear, and barred and locked the doors with jealous care, and even looked to the fastenings of the windows, and caught some faint shadows of that supernatural fear with which Alice Fairfield had come to regard the wicked woman out of whose hands she had escaped.

Now and then, when appealed to, she said a short word or two of re-assurance respecting Charles Fairfield's unaccountably prolonged absence. But the panic of the young lady in like manner on this point began to invade her in uncomfortable misgivings.

So uneasy had she grown that at last she dispatched Tom, when sunset had come without a sign of Charles Fairfield's return, riding to Wykeford. Tom had now returned. A bootless errand it had proved. At Wykeford he learned that Charles Fairfield had been there—had been at Squire Rodney's house and about the town, and made inquiries. His pursuit had been misdirected. At Wykeford is a House of Correction and Reformatory, which institution acts as a prison of ease to the county jail. But that jail is in the town of Hatherton, as Charles would have easily recollected if his rage had allowed him a moment to think. Tom, however, made no attempt further to pursue him, on conjecture, and had returned to Carwell Grange, no wiser than he went.

CHAPTER XIX.

CHARLES FAIRFIELD, in true Fairfield wrath, had ridden at a hard pace, which helped to keep his blood up, all the way to the bridge of Wykeford. He had expected to overtake the magistrate easily before he reached that point, and if he had, who knows what might have happened next.

Baulked at Wykeford, and learning there how long a ride interposed before he could hope to reach him, he turned and followed in a somewhat changed mood.

He would himself bail that woman. The question, felony or no felony—bailable offence or not bailable—entered not his uninstructed head. Be she what she might, assassin— devil, he could not and would not permit her to lie in jail. Arrested in his own house, with many sufferings and one great wrong to upbraid him with—with rights, imaginary he insisted, but honestly believed in, perhaps, by her—with other rights, which his tortured heart could not deny, the melancholy rights which are founded on outlawry and disgrace, eleemosynary, but quite irresistible when pleaded with natures not lost to all good, and which proclaim the dreadful equity—that vice has its duties no less than virtue.

Baulked in his first violent impulse, Charles rode his hot horse quietly along the by-road that leads to Hatherton, over many a steep and through many a rut.

Yes, pleasant it would have been to "lick" that rascal Rodney, and upset his dog-cart into the ditch, and liberate the distressed damsel. But even Charles Fairfield began to perceive consequences, and to approve a more moderate course.

At Hatherton was there not Peregrine Hincks, the attorney who carried his brother,

Harry Fairfield, whose course, any more than that of true love, did not always run smooth, through the short turns and breaks that disturbed it ?

He would go straight to this artist in all manner of quips and cranks in parchment, and tell him what he wanted—the most foolish thing perhaps in the world, to undo that which his good fortune had done for him, and let loose again his trouble.

Scandal ! What did the defiant soul of a Fairfield care for scandal ? Impulsive, reckless, affectionate, not ungenerous—all considerations were lost in the one compunctious feeling.

Two hours later he was in the office of Mr. Peregrine Hincks, who listened to his statement with a shrewd inflexibility of face. He knew as much as Harry Fairfield did of the person who was now under the turnkey's tutelage. But Charles fancied him quite in the dark, and treated the subject accordingly.

" We'll send down to the jail, and learn what she's committed for, but *two* will be necessary. Who will execute the recognizance with you ? "

" I'm certain Harry will do it in a moment," said Charles.

The attorney was very sure that Harry would do no such thing. But it was not necessary to discuss that particular point, nor to insinuate officiously his ideas about the county scandal which would follow his interposition in favour of a prisoner committed upon a charge involving an attempt upon the life of his wife, for the information brought back from the prison was such as to convince the attorney that bail could not be accepted in the case.

On learning this, Charles' wrath returned. He stood for a time at the chimney-piece, examining in silence a candlestick that stood there, and then to the window he went, with a haggard, angry face, and looked out for a while with his hands in his pockets.

"Very well. So much the worse for Rodney," said he suddenly. "I told you my sole motive was to snub that fellow. He chose to make an arrest in my house —his d——d impertinence !—without the slightest reference to me, and I made up my mind, if I could, to let his prisoner go. That fellow wants to be kicked—I don't care twopence about anything else, but it's all one—I'll find some other way."

"You'd better have a glass of sherry, sir ; you're a little tired, and a biscuit."

"I'll have nothing, thanks, till I—till I— what was I going to say ? Time enough ; I have lots to do at home—a great deal, Mr. Hincks—and my head aches. I *am* tired, but I won't mind the wine, thank you, my head is too bad. If I could just clear it of two or three things I'd be all right, and rest a little. I've been overworked, and I'll ride over here to-morrow—that will do—and we'll talk it over ; and I don't choose the wretched, crazy woman to be shut up in prison, because that stupid prig, Rodney, pleases to say she's sane, and would like to hang her, just because she was arrested at Carwell ; and—and as you say, of course, if she is insane she is best out of the way ; but there are ways of doing things, and I won't be bullied by that vulgar snob. By —— if I had caught him to-day I'd have broken his neck, I believe."

" Glad you did *not* meet him, sir—a row at any time brings one into mischief, but an interference with the course of law—don't you see—a very serious affair, indeed ! "

" Well, see—yes, I suppose so, and there was just another thing. Believing, as I do, that wretched person quite mad—don't you see ?—it would be very hard to let her—to let her half starve there where they've put her—don't you think ?—and I don't care to go down to the place there, and all that ; and if you'd just manage to let her have this— it's all I can do just now—but—but its happening at my house—although I'm not a bit to blame, puts it on me in a way, and I think I can't do less than this."

He handed a bank-note to the attorney, and was looking all the time on a brief that lay on the table.

Mr. Hincks, the respectable attorney, was a little shy, also, as he took it.

"I'm to say you send it to—what's her name, by-the-by?" he asked.

"Bertha Velderkaust, but you need not mention me—only say it was sent to her—that's all. I'm so vexed, because as you may suppose, I had particular reasons for wishing to keep quiet, and I was staying there at the Grange, you know—Carwell—and thought I might keep quiet for a few weeks; and that wretched maniac comes down there while I was for a few days absent, and in one of her fits makes an attack on a member of my family; and so my little hiding place is disclosed, for of course such a fracas will be heard of, — it is awfully provoking — I'm rather puzzled to know where to go."

Charles ceased, with a faint, dreary laugh, and the attorney looked at his bank-note, which he held by the corners, as the mate, in Mudford's fine story, might at the letter which Vanderdecken wished to send to his long-lost wife in Amsterdam.

It was not, however, clear to him that he had any very good excuse for refusing to do this trifling kindness for the brother of his quarrelsome and litigious client, Harry Fairfield, who, although he eschewed costs himself, laid them pretty heavily upon others, and was a valuable feeder for Mr. Hincks' office.

This little commission, therefore, accepted, the attorney saw his visitor downstairs. He had already lighted a candle, and in its light he thought he never saw a man upon his legs look so ill as Charles, and the hand which he gave Mr. Hincks at the steps was dry and burning.

"It's a long ride, sir, to Carwell," the attorney hesitated.

"The horse has had some oats, thanks, down here," and he nodded toward the Plume of Feathers at which he had put up his beast, "and I shan't be long getting over the ground."

And without turning about, or a look over his shoulder, he sauntered away, in the rising moonlight, toward the little inn.

CHAPTER XX.

CHARLES rode his horse slowly homeward. The moon got up before he reached the wild expanse of Cressley Common, a wide sea of undulating heath, with here and there a grey stone peeping above its surface in the moonlight like a distant sail.

Charles was feverish—worn out in body and mind—literally. Some men more than others are framed to endure misery, and live on, and on, and on in despair. Is this melancholy strength better, or the weakness that faints under the first strain of the rack? Happy that at the longest it cannot be for very long—happy that "man that is born of a woman hath but a short time to live," seeing that he is "full of misery."

Charles was conscious only of extreme fatigue; that for days he had eaten little and rested little, and that his short snatches of sleep, harassed by the repetition of his waking calculations and horrors, tired rather than refreshed him.

When fever is brewing, just as electric lights glimmer from the sullen mask of cloud on the eve of a storm, there come sometimes odd flickerings that seem to mock and warn.

Every overworked man, who has been overtaken by fever in the midst of his toil and complications, knows well the kind of tricks his brain has played him on the verge of that chaos.

Charles put his hand to his breast, and felt in his pocket for a letter, the appearance of which was sharp and clear on his retina as if he had seen it but a moment before.

"What have I done with it?" he asked himself—"the letter Hincks gave me?"

He searched his pockets for it, a letter of

which this picture was so bright—purely
imaginary! He was going to turn about and
search the track he had traversed for it; but
he bethought him, "To whom was the letter
written?" No answer could he find. "To
whom?" To no one—nothing—an imagination. Conscious on a sudden, he was
scared.

"I want a good rest—I want some sleep
—waking dreams. This is the way fellows go
mad. What the devil can have put it into
my head?"

Now rose before him the tall trees that
gather as you approach the vale of Carwell,
and soon the steep gables and chimneys of
the Grange glimmered white among their
boughs.

There in his mind, as unaccountably, was
the fancy that he had met and spoken
with his father, old Squire Harry, at the Cat-
stone, as he crossed the moor.

"I'll give his message—yes, I'll give your
message."

And he thought what possessed him to come out without his hat, and he looked whiter than ever.

And then he thought, " What brought him there ? "

And then, " What *was* his message ? "

Again a shock, a chasm—his brain had mocked him.

Dreadful when that potent servant begins to mutiny, and instead of honest work for its master finds pastime for itself in fearful sport.

"My God! what am I thinking of ? " he said, with a kind of chill, looking back over his shoulder.

His tired horse was plucking a mouthful of grass that grew at the foot of a tree.

"We are both used up," he said, letting his horse, at a quicker pace, pursue its homeward path. " Poor fellow, you are tired as well as I. I'll be all right, I dare say, in the morning if I could only sleep. Something wrong—something a little wrong—that sleep will cure—all right to-morrow."

He looked up as he passed toward the windows of his and Alice's room. When he was out a piece of the shutter was always open. But if so to-night there was no light in the room, and with a shock and a dreadful imperfection of recollection, the scene which occurred on the night past returned.

"Yes, my God! so it was," he said, as he stopped at the yard gate. "Alice—I forget —did I see Alice after that, did I—did they tell me—what is it?"

He dismounted, and felt as if he were going to faint. His finger was on the latch, but he had not courage to raise it. Vain was his effort to remember. Painted in hues of light was that dreadful crisis before his eyes, but how had it ended? Was he going quite mad?"

"My God help me," he muttered again and again. "Is there anything bad. I can't recall it. Is there anything very bad?"

"Open the door, it is he, I'm sure, I heard the horse," cried the clear voice of Alice from within.

"Yes, I, it's I," he cried in a strange rapture.

And in another moment the door was open, and Charles had clasped his wife to his heart.

"Darling, darling, I'm so glad. You're quite well?" he almost sobbed.

"Oh, Ry, my own, my own husband, my Ry, he's safe, he's quite well. Come in. Thank God, he's back again with his poor little wife, and oh, darling, we'll never part again. Come in, come in, my darling."

Old Mildred secured the door, and Tom took the horse round to the stable, and as she held her husband clasped in her arms, tears, long denied to her, came to her relief, and she wept long and convulsingly.

"Oh, Ry, it has been such a dreadful time; but you're safe, aren't you?"

"Quite. Oh! yes, quite darling—very well."

" But, oh, Ry, you look so tired. You're not ill, are you, darling ? "

" Not ill, only tired. Nothing, not much, tired and stupid, want of rest."

" You must have some wine, you look so very ill."

" Well, yes, I'm tired. Thanks, Mildred, that will do," and he drank the glass of sherry she gave him.

" A drop more ? " inquired old Mildred, holding the decanter stooped over his glass.

" No, thanks, no, I—it tastes oddly—or perhaps I'm not quite well after all."

Charles now felt his mind clear again, and his retrospect was uncrossed by those spectral illusions of the memory that seem to threaten the brain with subjugation.

Better the finger of death than of madness should touch his brain, perhaps. His love for his wife, not dethroned, only in abeyance, was restored. Such dialogues as theirs are little interesting to any but the interlocutors.

With their fear and pain, agitated, troubled, there is love in their words. Those words, then, though in him, troubled with inward upbraidings, in her with secret fears and cares, are precious. There may not be many more between them.

CHAPTER XXI.

THE WYKEFORD DOCTOR.

A FEW days had passed and a great change had come. Charles Fairfield, the master of the Grange, lay in his bed, and the Wykeford doctor admitted to Alice that he could not say what might happen. It was a very grave case—fever—and the patient could not have been worse handled in those early days of the attack, on which sometimes so much depends.

People went to and fro' on tiptoe, and talked in whispers, and the patient moaned, and prattled, unconscious generally of all that was passing. Awful hours and days of suspense! The Doctor said, and perhaps he was right, to kind Lady Wyndale, who came over to see Alice, and learned with consternation the state of things, that, under the special circumstances, her nerves having been so violently acted upon by terror, this diversion of pain and thought into quite another channel might be the best thing, on the whole, that could have happened to her.

It was now the sixth day of this undetermined ordeal.

Alice watched the Doctor's countenance with her very soul in her eyes, as he made his inspection, standing at the bed-side, and now and then putting a question to Dulcibella or to Alice, or to the nurse whom he had sent to do duty in the sick-room from Wykeford.

"Well?" whispered poor Alice, who had accompanied him downstairs, and pale as death, drew him into the sitting-room, and asked her question.

"Well, Doctor, what do you think to-day?"

"Not much to report. Very little change. We must have patience, you know, for a day or two; and you need not to be told, my dear ma'am, that good nursing is half the battle, and in better hands he need not be; I'm only afraid that you are undertaking too much yourself. That woman, Marks, you may rely upon, implicitly; a most respectable and intelligent person; I never knew her to make a mistake yet, and she has been more than ten years at this work."

"Yes, I'm sure she is. I like her very much. And don't you think him a little better?" she pleaded.

"Well, you know, as long as he holds his own and don't lose ground, he *is* better; that's all we can say; not to be worse, as time elapses, is in effect, to be better; that you *may* say."

She was looking earnestly into the clear blue eyes of the old man, who turned them kindly upon her, from under his shaggy white eyebrows.

"Oh! thank God, then you do think him better?"

"In that sense, yes," he answered cautiously, "but, of course, we must have patience, and we shall soon know more, a great deal more, and I do sincerely hope it may all turn out quite right; but the brain has been a good deal overpowered; there's a tendency to a sort of state we call comatose; it indicates too much pressure there, d'ye see. I'd rather have him talking more nonsense, with less of that sleep, as you suppose it, but it isn't sleep,—a very different sort of thing. I've been trying to salivate him, but he's plaguy obstinate. We'll try to-night what dividing the pills into four each, and shortening the intervals a little will do; it sometimes does wonders—we'll see—and a great deal depends on our succeeding in salivating. If we succeeded in effecting that, I think all the rest would proceed satisfactorily, that's one of our difficulties just at this moment. If you send over your little messenger, the sooner the better, she shall have the pills, and let him take one the moment they come—pretty flower that is," he interpolated, touching the petal of one that stood neglected, in its pot, on a little table at the window. "That's not a geranium : it's a pelargonium. I did not know there were such things down here—and you'll continue, I told her everything else, and go on just as before."

"And you think he's better—I mean just a little ?" she pleaded again.

"Well, well, you know, I said all I could, and we must hope—we must hope, you know, that everything may go on satisfactorily, and I'll go further. I'll say I don't see at all why we should despair of such a result. Keep up your spirits, ma'am, and be cheery. We'll do our duty all, and leave the rest in the hands of God."

"And I suppose, Dr. Willett, we shall see you to-morrow at the usual hour ? "

"Certainly, ma'am, and I don't think there will be any change to speak of till, probably, Thursday."

And her heart sank down with one dreadful dive at mention of that day of trial that might so easily be a day of doom.

And she answered his farewell, and smiled faintly, and followed his steps through the passage, freezing with that fear, it seemed, that she did not breathe, and that her heart ceased beating, and that she glided like a spirit. She stopped, and he passed into the yard to his horse, turning his shrewd, pale face, with a smile and a nod, as he stepped across the door-stone, and he said—

"Good-bye, ma'am, and look out for me to-morrow as usual, and be cheery, mind. Look at the bright side, you know ; there's no reason you shouldn't."

She answered his smile as best she could, but her heart was full ; an immense sorrow was there. She was frightened. She hurried into the homely sitting-room, and wept in an agony unspeakable.

The doctor, she saw, pitied and wished to cheer her ; but how dreadful was his guarded language. She thought that he would speak to others in a different vein, and so, in fact, he did. His opinion was clear against Charles

Fairfield's chance of ever being on his feet again. "It was a great pity — a young fellow." The doctor thought everyone young whose years were ten less than his own. "A tall, handsome fellow like that, and Squire of Wyvern in a year or two, and a good-natured sort of fellow he heard. It was a pity, and that poor little wife of his— and likely to be a mother soon—God help her."

THE END OF VOL II.

BRADBURY, EVANS, AND CO., PRINTERS, WHITEFRIARS.